Anointed Inspirations Publishing

Presents

You Thought He Was Yours

A novel by

Denora M. Boone

Published by Anointed Inspirations Publishing

Anointed Inspirations Publishing is currently accepting Urban Christian Fiction, Inspirational Romance, and Young Adult fiction submissions. For consideration please send manuscripts to
Anointedinspirationspublishing@gmail.com

Connect with Denora Socially
Facebook: www.facebook.com/AuthorDenora
Twitter: www.twitter.com/mzboone27
Instagram: @mzboone81
www.authordenora.com

CK

-1-

Trinity watched as her husband Bless moved around the room with a sneer plastered on her face. It wasn't that she was disgusted with his appearance because he was one of the finest men she had ever met. That was one of the reasons she got with him in the first place. But his ambition wasn't hitting on nothing.

Standing at 6'4" and weighing almost 270 pounds, Bless was a smooth chocolate complexion with dark brown eyes and the deepest set of dimples she had ever seen on a man. The way his long dreads hung down his back gave him that Rastafarian look that the women loved but unfortunately it did nothing for her anymore. If she had to compare him to anyone it would be Pittsburgh Steelers linebacker Alvin "Bud" Dupree. Now if only he had the deep pockets like Bud all would be well in her world but he didn't. Instead he wanted to work a minimum wage job at a convenience store with the hopes of owning a few one day. To her that was just a poor man's dream and she didn't have time for that.

"I thought you were off today," Trinity said in an icy tone.

It was going on six in the morning on what was

supposed to be his off day and here he was about to head into work because someone was a no call no show. Bless would have loved to lay up with his wife of the last seven years and just talk to her about his dreams but he knew that would never happen. Anytime he would bring up the ideas or visions that he had she would brush him off or comment something that made him feel less than a man. This had been their same routine for the last five years of their marriage, yet he continued to pray that God would change her hardened heart.

Trinity was gorgeous but sometimes the things she said or would do made her look evil. Still no matter what she was his wife and he loved her. She was on the thin side but not in a way that made her look sick. Her real hair wasn't extremely long but no one would ever know because of all of the weave that she wore. Her makeup stayed flawless and she wouldn't dare leave the house without it. No matter how many times he would compliment her on her natural beauty she would shut him down and accuse him of trying to control what she wore. That wasn't the case and he could never figure out how she thought him complimenting her was his way of controlling her.

"I was off but no one showed up to relieve Autumn so I have to go in," he told her as he tucked in his work shirt. His body and mind were both operating off of only four hours of sleep and he didn't feel like arguing at that moment. Trinity on the other hand lived to argue with him.

"I bet. You're probably just using that as an excuse to be all up in her face," Trinity sucked her teeth and removed the comforter from her beautiful body before walking into the master bathroom.

That was another thing that Bless wished she wouldn't do. Besides never believing in his dreams she was always accusing him of being with another woman. If no one else knew how serious he took his wedding vows it should have been her. Granted they didn't have enough for a big wedding but he made sure to put a lot of thought into their wedding day making it as special for her as possible. Unlike most men who played the background when it came to wedding planning he was the complete opposite. He was the one that picked the location, date, time, cake, the whole nine yards. All she had to do was show up.

Feeling like she was the one for him their sophomore year in college, he decided to make sure she had his last name before he got drafted into the NFL. Only that didn't happen. They had been married for two years at the time of his last game when he was hit with a career ending injury that cost him everything. Even his wife. In his heart he felt like the moment Trinity found out that he would no longer be going pro things for her changed. Still he knew that he served a mighty God that could turn any situation around. He just wondered how long it would take.

Bless' parents who were both ministers gave him as much advice as they could without being overbearing. When it came to how they felt personally about Trinity they put those personal feelings to the side and to him how he should work on his marriage. He was grateful for them and knew that the advice was sound advice but Trinity wanted no parts of it. They explained how both Bless and Trinity needed as much time together as possible so that the enemy didn't have room to slide in and pull them further apart. Bless had done everything he could to make sure he was available but his wife would always claim that she was too busy. Since she was a flight attendant for Delta she made sure to use that as an excuse. Yet he was still holding on to the idea of a healthy and happy marriage that God promised him.

"Baby you know there isn't anyone else. Why do you always do this when I have to work? I don't do that to you when you have to leave," he told her feeling himself becoming agitated.

"You call being at that gas station work? Boy bye. Want to know what's classified as real work? Work would be you out on someone's football field tackling people for an eight-figure salary," she spit with so much venom in her voice it would make a rattlesnake cringe.

Sighing Bless felt one of his familiar migraines surfacing and it wasn't even 7am.

"Trin you know that this is just the stepping stone for me opening my own chain of 7-11's so that neither of us will have to work for anyone else. We can finally spend more time together and begin working on starting a family."

The way her body tensed up didn't go unnoticed by Bless and he already knew what her response was going to be. It was the same one that she gave him each and every time he brought up them having children. She wasn't ready.

"B you know that I'm not ready for kids yet. We talked about this more than once and you told me that you would be patient," she stressed for the millionth time.

What Trinity really wanted to say was that she didn't want kids by *him*. There was no way that she would dare bring a baby into the world with a man like Bless. She could already see them now struggling to make ends meet all because of some pipe dream that would never come true. She wasn't about that life and no amount of love would make her change her mind. It didn't matter though because one day he would come home and find her gone and that day couldn't get there fast enough for her.

Feeling defeated yet again Bless decided to make his way to the store. Hopping in his 2006 Chevy Suburban he turned on some worship music and began to pray. Normally he would do that inside of his home but since Trinity had gotten him in such a sour mood he needed to remove himself from that environment in order to clear his head. He had spent a good fifteen minutes in the driveway with God before he realized that he needed to get going.

Just as he was backing out of the yard, Trinity came outside dressed in her uniform with her carryon bag and he didn't even have to ask her where she was going. The only thing he didn't know was when she would be returning so he decided to ask her.

"Baby how long will you be gone?" he asked before she could get into her car.

Each time he saw her brand new 2017 BMW he got angry. Bless had asked his wife many times to just wait a little longer and he would get her the car and house that she wanted but Trinity could be a spoiled brat at times and didn't listen. She felt like she could afford it because she made more money than he did but after a few months of her having it, he was the one that was made responsible for making the payments on it. He was so glad that his truck was paid for in full because her payments were almost triple what his would have been. The Suburban may not have been as luxurious as she wanted but it was his and he held the title.

"Don't know. I'll just see you when I get back," she told him with much attitude before hopping in and heading in the opposite direction Bless was going in.

"God if this is your will please fix it," Bless prayed before taking the twenty minute drive to work.

-2-

When Bless pulled up to the front of the store he hopped out and made his way inside. Autumn looked like she was ready to get out of there and he could totally understand it. He hated when he had to work overnight because it felt like the hours would drag by.

"I'm sorry boss for calling you on your off day. I would have stayed but my mama called to tell me that my granny had been rushed to the hospital," she explained to him.

Autumn was a sweet girl right out of high school. Her looks reminded him of that singer and actress Zendaya and she even had the same bubbly and kind personality. She would always go above and beyond for anything that she set her mind out to do. That was the main reason that after almost a year of working there she was promoted to assistant manager.

"What did I tell you about calling me boss? This isn't my store but you go ahead and check on your grandma. Let Ms. Lucy know I'm praying for her."

"I know it's not your store but it might as well be. No one else can run this place like you do so I know when you open your own there won't be any difference.

Anyway I'll let her know and thanks for understanding."

Since it was still a little dark outside Bless watched her to make sure she got safely in her car before pulling out of the lot. Looking around the store he could already tell that Autumn had stocked the shelves that needed more items added to them and made sure the money that needed to be deposited was where he could find it easily. This was exactly why the moment he opened his first store he was taking Autumn with him. At the rate she was going he knew that in a few years if she stuck it out with him she would be owning one of her own. He was all about helping to elevate the next person especially if he was in a position to do so. Bless may not have been there now but he knew that his time was coming.

Just as he had made it around to the back of the counter to place the deposit bag into the safe the door chimed causing him to speak before looking up.

"Good morning and welcome to 7-11," he called out.

"Good morning Bless," a familiar voice spoke.

It was definitely a good morning whenever he saw Anya O'Day come into his store which was every morning before she went to work. There were even some days he was lucky enough to see her when she got off and heading home. Something about her presence seemed to take away all of the stress that he was feeling whenever she came around and it was definitely welcomed.

Bless may have been married but he couldn't deny the person that she was. He knew that whenever her husband did find her he would be one lucky man. Anya was tall for a woman and a bit on the heavier side but it was all proportioned so well. She had a golden colored skin tone with pretty dark brown eyes. Her lashes were so long that they looked fake but he knew they were real. Unlike his wife, Anya wore her long hair natural and each time she came in her burgundy bush would be styled a different way giving her a fresh new look.

Today she had it piled on top of her head in a huge curly puff with a few strands falling out of her hair tie. The navy blue skirt she wore fit snug against her body but in a good way and the pair of strappy gold heels matched the shirt she was wearing. He could only imagine how her male coworkers at the real estate office felt being around her day in and day out.

Every time Anya came into the store she prayed that he would be working. It wasn't that she was wanting him but she genuinely loved being in his presence because of something more. Bless possessed something so powerful within him and it made her wonder if he was aware of it. That one thing was that he had the Holy Spirit dwelling inside of him and it was so strong. To her that was the sexiest thing that a man could ever possess.

A man that was after God's own heart was so attractive to her. That's why the moment that she saw him after all of those years had passed and noticed the wedding band on his finger, she knew that he would never step out on his marriage. Because of that she put her feelings that grew gradually over time to the back of her mind and repented for yearning for someone else's husband.

Anya would never forget the day that she met Bless in one of those online chat rooms when she was a freshman in high school. There was no Facebook, Instagram, or Snapchat back then so no one knew what the other person looked like unless they met face to face. She may have been confident in her appearance now but during those times her self-esteem was so low that it caused her to do things that she wasn't proud of. Some of the consequences that came from her actions had nearly cost Anya her life. They had conversed for almost a year then one day it all of a sudden stopped. She reached out to him multiple times but it was as if it Bless had fallen off the face of the earth. The was no way to explain how deep she had fallen for Bless by just their conversations so it hit her hard when he was no longer in communications with her. After a while she finally decided to give up and move on doing her best to forget the man that held her heart, then it happened.

The day that Anya had moved back to Minneapolis she had just gotten settled in and decided to run to the corner store for some snacks. Bless was behind the counter working hard and when he looked up into her face she felt like her breath was caught up between her lungs and throat barely making it out of her body. He spoke to her and she swore her legs were about to betray her and give out. Just as she imagined her body hitting the floor she saw the ring that rested on his finger. If nothing turned her off more it was a married man that wasn't married to her. She didn't want those kind of problems.

Going on about her business of picking up everything that she knew she didn't need, Anya finally made her way to the counter to pay. Bless greeted her and made small talk before handing her the bag. When he reached out to her she noticed the name tag that was on his red collar shirt. Looking at him long and hard it didn't take long for her to know that it was indeed *her* Bless. The description that he had given her of himself online when they were younger was dead on with just a few differences. His hair was a lot longer but she knew that he was the same person. Her heart knew it but her mind told her not to say anything. She wasn't worried about him knowing who she was because he didn't know her first name. Online she went by her middle name *'Manae'* and up until that moment she still hadn't revealed who she really was.

"What's up An," he replied bringing her back from

the past. His face was covered with one of the biggest grins that he always seemed to wear whenever she was around.

"On my way to the office as usual. I have an open house this afternoon," she told him.

"That's what's up. I know you got that sale so don't even trip. This all you need this morning?" he asked her referring to the two cups of coffee that she had made when she walked in.

"That's it. I know if I come in with one for me but not for Cassidy she's gonna have a fit," Anya laughed.

"Well since this is a big day for you these are on the house," he offered. The smile he gave her was genuine and that made her heart flutter.

Get yourself together girl! God gone close the gate on Judgement Day if you keep this up. She scolded herself while returning the warm smile.

"Thanks Bless. Let me go ahead and get out of here before I'm late. You have a blessed day," she told him grabbing the two cups just as the door chimed getting both of their attention.

"Oh so this why you were all in a hurry to get here?" a woman that Anya had never seen before said with nothing but malice in her voice. She was gorgeous in the looks department but her attitude and spirit made her ugly.

"Trinity you already know why I had to come in. Can we not do this here?"

Anya finally put two and two together and figured this may be his wife so she decided to cut their conversation short and make her way out. The last thing she wanted was to be brought into their marriage because of something that she wasn't even doing. She didn't know what the issues were that they were facing but she knew that it had to be serious. Especially if Bless was wearing his wedding ring but his wife wasn't.

"Thank you for the coffee and have a good day Bless. Excuse me," Anya spoke moving around Trinity.

"By all means don't let me interrupt you two," Trinity sneered.

Instead of responding Anya just walked out of the store and made her way back to her car. Trinity didn't even deserve a response from her. There was nothing between she and Bless no matter what his wife may have felt.

"Why do you always have to act like this at my job Trin? You know good and well that I'm not out here trying to be with anyone else but you. Why do you think I'm working so hard for us?"

"Whatever, I'm gone," she said turning on her

heels and walking back out.

Bless didn't even get the chance to ask her why she was there in the first place when she left home before him in the direction of the airport. That she was glad about because she wasn't about to tell him that she was off for the next week and was heading to her boyfriend's house. The only reason she had stopped to begin with was because as she was passing the store she saw that woman inside looking like she had stepped off a plus sized runway.

Trinity knew that she was a beauty but there was something about that woman that stood there talking to her husband that rubbed her the wrong way. Or maybe it was just her guilty conscious that made her show out the way she did. She wasted no time putting those feelings to rest as she made her way to spend the next week with her bae.

-3-

"What has you so deep in thought?" Cassidy asked Anya walking into her office.

Anya had been so unfocused since she left the store and Bless earlier. Her thoughts were all over the place and no matter how much she tried she just couldn't get it together.

"Oh nothing just thinking," Anya replied with a smile.

"I know that look in your eyes," Cassidy continued coming further into the office.

Cassidy had been her closest friend since moving to Minneapolis almost five years ago after leaving her then fiancé Nardo. The two of them shared so much with one another but there were just some things that Anya wanted to keep to herself at times. It irked Anya to no end that Cassidy could never pick up on when to leave well enough alone. Be it her body language, tone of voice, or even a roll of the eye, Cassidy ignored it all. But being really the only friend she had there, Anya never wanted to be mean and just flat out tell her to mind her business. So instead of hurting her friend's feelings she kept quiet. She just wished that Cassidy would one day get the picture loud and clear instead of continuing to say whatever was on her mind. No matter how blunt or hurtful it was. Some days it was easy to ignore but from the excitement on her girl's face she knew that today wasn't one of those days.

"What look Cass?"

"The one that is telling me your panties need to be changed. Who is he? Let me find out Nardo got himself together," Cassidy said excitedly making her way to the plush chair across from Anya.

That was another thing that bothered Anya about Cassidy. Her mouth was filthy. True enough they were both grown women but some things were just better left unsaid.

"Do you always have to be so nasty? What would Pastor say?" Anya smirked.

"He would probably tell me to hurry up and take mine off so he could handle his business," she laughed while sticking her tongue out and popping her butt in her seat. She was one of the most ratchet First Ladies Anya had ever met but made no apologies for it. The way Anya looked at it no matter how she felt Cass was going to do what Cass wanted so she kept her thoughts to herself.

"Ugh! Not something I wanted to visualize Cass. But to answer your question, no Marquee did not get himself together and there is no other man," she half told the truth.

Her ex Marquee didn't get himself together and even if he did she wouldn't go back to him. That was one toxic relationship that almost cost her her life and a lesson only had to be taught once for her to understand it. The lie that she did tell however, was that there was no other man on her mind. She kept kicking herself every time she visualized Bless smiling down at her with those deep dimples on full display with nothing but admiration in his eyes towards her.

"See there it is again. Girl who is it?" Cassidy asked in anticipation.

Going against her better judgement Anya caved in and filled her girl in.

"You know that 7-11 by my house?"

"The one you go to every morning where that fine dude with the dreads works?" Cassidy remembered before another thought came to her mind. "Oh unt uh honey. I know good and well you not feeling him. I mean he's fine as all get out but if he works there he can't have any real money. And didn't you tell me a while back that he was married? You know God does not care for side chicks," Cassidy rambled on as Anya rolled her eyes.

Says the woman who was the side chick before she

became the wife, Anya thought to herself.

Before becoming First Lady Cassidy Hightower she must have forgotten that she had been Side Chick number two to Pastor Leron Hightower. He was married with another girlfriend on the side when Cassidy met him and before long she had charmed him right out of the both of their arms and into hers. It wasn't for Anya to judge but that didn't mean that she agreed with it.

"And before you go there Ron was already going through a divorce before we started anything." Cassidy knew that was one of the biggest lies that she had ever told but Anya didn't need to know the details.

It was no secret that when Leron approached her that she should have run far away but she couldn't. He had swept her off her feet and she wasn't willing to leave him no matter what. His wife Heather was the ideal wife and first lady but she was boring as hell. No matter how spontaneous he needed her to be she was too timid and holier than thou. Cassidy already knew when he began telling her the issues in their marriage what she needed to do. Be a woman in the streets and a freak in the sheets! It took him some time to go through with the divorce but once it was final they were married the following week.

"If you say so Cass. Anyway I'm not trying to be an adulterer and have God send me a harvest that I don't want to reap. And why does how much money he has in his account matter? Marquee had money and you see how that ended up."

"Girl you sound stupid. How are you supposed to be with a man that doesn't even fall in the same tax bracket as you do? That's like taking care of a grown child and God clearly says in His word that the man is the provider and covering for his family," Cassidy explained.

Anya was amazed at how so many people could pick the Bible apart to fit what they wanted it to instead of for what it really was. Being that she knew and understood a man was to be his family's covering she still felt like if he was to fall on hard times then she was to be his help meet. Especially if he was trying his best and trusting God.

Instead of getting into that debate once again with Cass she decided to head on over to the house that she was showing. The longer she sat still the more she was going to be in her thoughts or sitting there listening to Cassidy talk crazy.

"Let me get up out of here and get over to this house. My new client has a baby on the way and needs something bigger," Anya told her as she stood from her chair and began grabbing her things. She had about another three hours before they were meeting but she didn't care. It was time to go.

"Well let me know how it goes. I have one tomorrow that I need to prep for. You coming to Bible study tonight?" Cassidy wondered.

"Nah not this time but soon," Anya replied just like she normally did.

Mt. Olive Baptist church wasn't a bad church to attend it just wasn't for Anya. She knew that all churches had their fair share of mess and weren't perfect but Mt. Olive took that to a whole new level. Besides the fact that she wasn't getting fed spiritually her ex still attended that church. So instead of putting herself in a tough situation she backed off going. Sure God wanted her to be able to fellowship with other believers but He also gave her a strong gift of discernment. That wasn't the place that He wanted her and in due time she was confident she would find the right church home.

"Ok then boo call me later," Cassidy told her before leaving her office and returning to her own. Normally she would have kept pushing so Anya was pleased that she didn't. Grabbing her purse, phone, and briefcase Anya locked up and headed off to hopefully have another successful sale on her resume.

***

It was just before two in the afternoon and Anya knew that her client would be arriving any minute to see the house that she had found just for him. Emmanuel Dennis was a well-known real estate investor in Minneapolis and there was no limit on how much he wanted to spend on his next house. Emmanuel spent most of his time traveling to different places because his job required it but now that he was about to have a family of his own he wanted to have a place that was just for them. In Anya's opinion this was the perfect home for them.

She had just finished going over her paperwork when she heard someone enter the house through the front door.

"Hello?" a familiar deep baritone voice called out.

Instantly she made her presence known from the state of the art kitchen that she stood in. There was no doubt in her mind that Mrs. Dennis would fall head over heels in love with it. From the information that she had gathered from Emmanuel, his better half lived in the kitchen cooking up new dishes for him. His main request was that the house Anya found for him would be one with a kitchen like no other.

"Good afternoon Mr. Dennis," Anya spoke as she rounded the corner almost bumping right into him.

"Now what have I told you about calling me that?" Emmanuel smiled at her.

"I'm sorry it's just out of respect for my clients. I try to remain professional at all times."

"I understand and I appreciate that. Not all women have that mindset," he told her.

For him to be older than she was there was no way that she could deny the handsome man that stood in front of her. That's why she understood exactly what he meant by that comment he had just made. He wasn't extremely tall, maybe six foot even, he was slim but Anya could tell that he worked out a lot. Emmanuel had skin the color of sandpaper with funny looking green eyes. The way his salt and pepper hair and beard blended perfectly against his skin tone she was sure that most women would throw themselves at him. She just wasn't one of them. He was handsome but there was something about him that she had picked up in her spirit. She couldn't put her finger on it right away so she decided not to dwell on it and begin showing him his new home.

"You have really amazed me Anya. Now I see why my partner suggested that I come and see you. I was sure that I would need to see more than one house but there is no need to. This is the one," he praised her as he stood on the back balcony looking out over the huge backyard.

The massive four bedroom home that had six bathrooms and over five thousand square feet was just what he had been looking for. There was enough space for his growing family and he couldn't wait until they were all moved in.

"I'm glad that you approve Mr. Dennis. Would you like to take the papers with you to look over with your wife before signing?" Anya asked. Although she wanted him to just sign the papers so that she could go ahead and get the ball rolling she didn't want to seem too eager. That commission that she would receive would definitely be nice but she wasn't pressed for it.

"No need. I know that she will love it just as much as I do. Where do I sign?"

On the inside Anya was doing her best shout unto the Lord but on the outside she smiled politely and pulled out the necessary papers. It took her about ten minutes to go over everything before he gladly signed his John Hancock on the signature line.

"Well now that I have everything that I need I will contact the seller with your offer and we will hopefully have you moved in here soon," Anya let him know before placing everything back into her briefcase.

"I look forward to it. If they don't accept my offer you have my permission to give them a higher figure if needed. I'm not sparing any cost for this house," he said stunning her. Never had a client given her that type of authority but Anya was fair. If the seller wanted more money she had no problem giving a figure that would make all parties happy. She wasn't about to use this as a way to get over on someone like she knew other agents probably would. She never had been a shrewd business woman and she wasn't about to start now.

"Will do Mr. Dennis. You have a blessed weekend and I will contact you as soon as I have a reply."

Shaking one another's hand they both headed to their cars before Emmanuel stopped her again.

"Oh wait Anya. There was something that I needed to ask of you."

"Sure what is it?" she asked as she placed her belongings into her car and gave him her undivided attention.

"I have this one property that I am looking to get rid of but it hasn't piqued anyone's attention just yet. If I send over some pics and all of the other information would you mind listing it for me. The last realtor that I used wasn't doing what I needed them to do but being here with you and seeing how great of an agent you are I thought I'd ask."

"Absolutely I wouldn't mind at all. Thank you so much for the opportunity. As soon as you send everything over I'll get right on it," she assured him.

The two of them said their finally goodbyes and both headed off in different directions. Being that the house she had found was a little outside of Minneapolis in Minnetonka she knew that at this time of day traffic may have been a little hectic so she connected her Bluetooth to her radio and enjoyed the smooth sounds of Tink as she thanked God for yet another blessing.

-4-

"What's good bro?" Bless' best friend Terrell greeted him walking into the store.

Bless and Terrell had been best friends since they came out of the womb. Both of their mothers had grown up together and made sure to raise their boys the same way. If you saw one you saw the other and if one got in trouble they both took the fall. There was nothing that they didn't tell one another and rarely did they disagree. On the times they did disagree it was about the same thing, Trinity.

Terrell felt like from the gate she wasn't the one for his boy but Bless had blinders on when it came to her. Everybody around him could see the mistake that was being made when they first met except Bless. His heart was so big and he wanted to share it with someone the way that he saw his father share his love with his mother that everything Trinity showed him was law. After so many times of trying to make Bless aware of what she was doing he just gave up. Not that he wanted to but because God had instructed him to move out of the way.

There were so many times that people felt like they were doing a good deed for someone else but it wasn't what God wanted. Daily they would try to help by stepping in not thinking that what they were doing could backfire. It took some time but Terrell finally got the message loud and clear so he backed off. His friendship and brotherhood was more important than anything so he let Bless be. He and his wife Ronda prayed day in and day out that when Trinity was exposed that Bless' heart would be protected and wouldn't grow hard towards women. Bless had more than enough love to give but only for the right one.

"Man I'm tired bro," Bless said before letting out a yawn. It was going on five in the evening and because he had only gotten a few hours of sleep before getting the call to come in, his body was beginning to shut down.

"You look like it. What time you get off?" Terrell asked walking over to the drink section and grabbing a cherry vanilla Pepsi and an apple juice.

"I wasn't supposed to be here in the first place. I was off today but I'm just waiting on Reggie to get here so I can go shower and head over to the church," Bless let him know.

"That's wassup. I'm gonna run this stuff home to Ronda before she has a fit then I'll head over myself."

"Sis not going?" Blessed asked ringing up the items that Terrell had placed on the counter.

"Nah she went to her appointment earlier and the doctor put her on bed rest because she's already dilated two centimeters."

Ronda was just a little over 34 weeks pregnant with their first daughter and they were so excited. Bless was excited as well to meet his niece but there was a place in his heart that craved to have what his friend was living.

"My little princess trying to come already so she can have you wrapped around her little finger huh?" Bless laughed.

"You already know and I can't wait. But don't think she not gonna have her uncle wrapped around the other finger."

"That's right and she's gonna be spoiled to death by her aunt and I."

"Yeah well...," Terrell began but let his sentence fall off. Now wasn't the time that he wanted to talk about Trinity and Bless could see the frustration all over his face.

Before he could reply to Terrell his attention was directed elsewhere and was focused on the car that had just pulled up outside. Terrell didn't know who it was that was pulling up but whoever it was had his boy showing all 32 of his pearly white teeth. Returning his attention to the car they both watched as Anya got out of the car and walked towards the front.

"Who that?" Terrell wanted to know.

"Oh she's just a customer that comes in here on the regular," he replied never taking his eyes off of her or dropping his smile.

"Looks to me she bout to be family," Terrell joked.

"You know better than that bro. I'm married already and only have eyes for my wife."

"Who you trying to convince? Me or you?"

Bless knew it was a valid question coming from his friend but still he blew it off. They had been down this road plenty of times and he was still standing firm in what he believed in. Neither of them had time to continue talking because Anya had finally made her way to the door and stepped inside. Even with her heels from earlier replaced with some ballerina flats and her hair that was now down she was still flawless. He admired how unconcerned she was with constantly looking like she stepped off a runway but not to where she looked like a slob. In Trinity's eyes, she had to be dressed to the nines with a face full of makeup just to go to the grocery store. On many occasions Bless told her how beautiful she was naturally and she didn't need it but his praises fell on deaf ears.

"You still here?" she asked smiling at the two of them when she got to the counter.

Terrell stood back and watched the interaction between the two of them and it tripped him out how they were acting like they were the only two people in the room. He couldn't help but to smile because the connection was a familiar one. He knew it well considering it was the same one he shared with his wife.

"Ahem," Terrell cleared his throat reminding them that he was there.

"Oh my bad bro. Anya this is my best friend and brother Terrell. Bro this is my…umm..I mean Anya," Bless stammered. He didn't know what was coming over him but by the amused look on Terrell's face he knew that they would be having a talk later.

"Your what?" Terrell asked clearly enjoying making his boy squirm.

"Oh I'm just his friend but it's nice to meet you Terrell," Anya smiled before walking away towards the snack section. It took everything in her not to smile when Bless got tongued tied about who she was to him.

"Man bro she the one," Terrell told his friend while admiring the beauty that had stolen Bless' heart. He may not have seen it but it was loud and clear for Terrell.

"Yo you trippin'. You know I'm married," Bless defended.

"Not for long," Terrell mumbled. Bless heard him but decided not to speak on it.

"How did the open house go?" Blessed Anya once she got back to the counter.

"It went great. I didn't even have to show the whole house because as soon as my client saw it he knew that it was the one for his family. We close next week hopefully if these numbers are right for both parties," Anya explained excitedly. The passion for what she did was evident and he understood exactly how she was feeling because he felt the same way when he thought about being a store owner.

"You a real estate agent?" Terrell asked her.

"One of the best," Bless stepped in and said before he could catch himself.

That one comment gave Anya so many butterflies and made her heart skip two beats. The way he praised and encouraged her was nothing like she had ever experienced and she welcomed it.

"Thanks Bless I appreciate that. But yes I am. Are you looking to buy?" Anya inquired turning to Terrell.

"Not right now but I'm sure there are a few people

down at our church who may be interested. You should come to our career fair tomorrow. There will be a lot of other vendors as well as employers there and it could help you to reach some new buyers."

Bless knew what Terrell was doing and a part of him was happy that he had mentioned it first. He had been debating talking to her about it because he didn't want to give her the wrong impression or lead her on in any kind of way. So for it to come from someone else made him breathe a little easier.

"I would love to. Thank you for letting me know. What church and what time?" she asked.

"He Made a Way Tabernacle at ten."

"That's different," Anya spoke.

"Yeah my parents wanted to do something new. Stepping outside of the box when it comes to religion and focusing more on the spiritual and having a solid relationship with God," Bless informed her.

"Now that's what I need," Anya replied. She longed to find a church that wasn't full of theatrics and tradition. She needed one that would help her to continue building her relationship with God. There had been a few times that she had gone to different churches and as soon as she stepped inside she knew that God was nowhere near that place. Anya's discernment was strong and that was the reason that she was skeptical of certain things. So having a church home was very important to her.

"Well when you come trust and believe you won't want to leave. But let me get out of here and head home to Ronda. I'll see you tomorrow and it was nice meeting you Anya," Terrell said before he dapped up Bless and gave Anya a half hug.

The two of them may not have known what was about to happen but Terrell was no fool. He knew that something was brewing and he just prayed that they would allow God to just have His way as far as they were concerned. The both of them had already done things their way and it didn't work so now it was time for them to remove themselves and let God be God.

-5-

“Hello?” Bless answered his phone groggily. He was so sleepy that he didn’t even bother to open his eyes to see who it was calling.

“I know you are not still in the bed,” he heard his mother say on the other end.

“Yeah ma I’m beat. I pulled a double yesterday and then once I left church I stayed up until five this morning waiting on Trinity to call to let me know she made it to her destination safely.”

The sound of his mother Geneva sucking her teeth let him know that she was irritated with Trinity’s actions but he hoped that she would keep those thoughts to herself until he got a few more hours of sleep.

“Well get on up because you’re late and it’s someone here that I think can help guide you towards opening the store,” she told him.

“Ma it’s still dark outside so how can I be late? You been dippin’ in that communion wine again?” he teased her.

“Boy don’t play with me you know I’m a Henny kind of girl,” Geneva laughed.

“Ma!” Bless burst out laughing along with her.

"What you know about that Hen?"

"Um I haven't been saved all my life. Remember that," she told him playfully in spite of her feeling sorry for him.

Day in and day out since the first time that she and her husband met Trinity they had told him that she wasn't the one but he wouldn't listen. His heart was so big and he yearned to have that loving family that had been afforded to him. Bless was a blessing to his parents and they made sure that he knew that. They understood his need and desire but they also understood God's perfect timing and Trinity wasn't the one. As much as they tried to warn him he didn't listen so they backed off. Now here they were seven years later watching their son being taken advantage of but their hands were tied. This was something that he would have to learn on his own and she knew that it was going to take something drastic to open his eyes. Geneva just prayed that he was strong enough to endure it.

"Come on it's almost nine and you know the event starts at ten," she reminded him.

Groaning, Bless turned over and that was when he realized why it was still dark. His head was buried so deep under the covers and his pillow that the pitch blackness that surrounded him made him think that it was still nighttime.

"Oh shoot ma my bad," he apologized while throwing the cover off of him and letting the light assault his eyes.

"Mmm hmm well hurry up and come on. There's someone here that I think may be able to help you find a location for when you're ready to start the process of working on your store."

"Aiight give me a few and I will be right there. I'm sorry again ma," Bless said sincerely. He knew this even was important to his family and the church and the last thing he wanted was to not be there and show his support.

"Stop that baby there are no apologies needed. See you in a bit and I love you baby," Geneva reassured him before ending their call.

Bless stretched his toned arms above his head and headed to the bathroom to get himself clean and ready for his day. He knew that he needed to put a move on it so that he could go be in place to help in any capacity that he could. His body and mind were both tired but this was bigger than him. They had already anticipated for there to be well over a thousand people there for the career fair not including the many vendors and employers that would be on site. This one event could open up so many jobs for the people that were in need of one and he was glad that God had given this particular vision to his parents.

It took Bless less than thirty minutes to get showered and dressed in a red button down shirt, black slacks, and a pair of his favorite leather black Gucci loafers that his parents had given him for Christmas. It was the only pair of expensive shoes that he owned all because he felt like his money could be saved or used elsewhere. His parents understood where he was coming from and that was the main reason that they had given the shoes to him. They felt like he deserved that and so much more and wanted to treat their only son to something nice. Considering his wife never did.

Thinking of his wife while he pulled his long hair back into a ponytail it crossed his mind that he didn't know where she was. He hated that feeling and would always let her know that he worried about her when she was away. He wasn't doing it to keep tabs on her like she thought but even when she was away he wanted to be able to protect her. Anything could happen to her when she was alone and that was one of his greatest fears. He would always consider her when he would check in and although she never seemed to care one way or the other he did it anyway.

Just as he was putting on his watch, another gift from his parents, he heard the front door open. Alarm set in because no one else lived there but the two of them and though his parents along with Terrell and Ronda had keys for emergencies they would call before coming over. To hear someone in the house knowing there shouldn't be caused him to reach into his top drawer beside the bed and pull out his gun.

"Yeah I know where I left it," Bless heard Trinity whisper as they both came around the corner at the same time.

"Oh shoot! H-hey babe," Trinity stuttered out when she noticed that Bless stood before her with a gun aimed at her.

Bless should have been happy that his wife was indeed alright but too many red flags were going up and he wasn't sure why. The main one should have been the fact that she was home instead of working but ironically he could only focus on her calling him "babe." As much as he wanted to rejoice because it had been so long since she showed him any form of love and affection he couldn't. Something was up and he wanted to know just what it was.

"What are you doing here?" he questioned lowering his gun.

"Um excuse you? The last time that I checked I lived here too," she spat.

Not waiting on a response from him she moved around and headed into the guest bathroom. Bless figured that she had to use it so he waited until she came out a few moments later to say anything further.

"Man what?" Trinity sucked her teeth when she opened the door and saw him waiting for her. She was not in the mood to hear his whining or answer any of the other questions that he had to ask her. She came for one thing and now that she had gotten it she was ready to leave.

"I've been worried sick about you. You didn't call me and let me know that you made it to work yesterday," he told her.

"How many times do I have to tell you that I am not a child and you are not my daddy? I'm grown as hell and don't need to check in with anybody."

"I'm not saying it like that Trin. You know I just want to make sure you are always good," he responded defeated.

"Well as you can see I'm alive and well now move before I miss my flight. And if you must know my flight was cancelled until today," she lied. Unbeknownst to Bless she had the next three days off but he didn't need to know that.

Right before she got to the front door she stopped dead in her tracks turning around to face Bless. Looking him over she saw that he wasn't in his work clothes and looked way too good to be just sitting around the house. He was headed out and she could bet money that the reason he was so worried about where she was because he was about to get into something.

"While you worried about me so much where are you going? I know it's not to work so what side piece you getting ready to go and see?"

Once again she was accusing him of doing something that had never crossed his mind to do just to take the heat off of her.

"Side piece? You can't be serious."

"As a heart attack," she told him while crossing her arms over her chest.

"I'm heading over to the church for the career fair. Since your flight was cancelled if you have time before you need to be back why don't you come with me?"

"Nah I have to go and make sure that if the flight become available again I'm right there. I just came back because I left my passport by mistake."

Something inside of him was telling him that she was lying but he couldn't be for sure. If she was there for her passport why was it in the bathroom? So many questions and not enough answers but neither of them had time for him to continue his inquiry.

"Well be safe and please call me when you get there." Bless offered up a smile while moving closer to her. "Can I get a kiss?" he asked her.

Quickly she pecked his cheek and swiftly made her moved back to the front. It felt like Bless' heart was once again breaking and it was becoming more and more clear by the day that he was losing his wife. He watched her get into her car with not even a glance back at him before she pulled off down the street.

"God please fix this marriage. I don't want to lose my wife," he said aloud. Taking a deep breath and blowing it out Bless stepped out of his door locking it behind him and making his way over to the church to help change some people's lives.

-6-

It took Bless about twenty minutes to get to the church that he had grown up in. He didn't know what was going on to have everybody out so early on a Saturday but traffic was thick. When he pulled up the parking lot was full of people causing him to smile. He loved to see when people got together for these type of events in order to bless and help God's people.

After parking in his designated parking space, Bless got out and looked around at all of the booths that were set up hoping to see one of his parents. Instead he spotted Terrell and Ronda at her booth selling her organic hair care products. She had so many people from that church that were requesting her products after the first event that she had attended that she finally decided to step out on faith and start her own business. It was one of the best decisions that she had ever made and now that she was about to be a mother she could still run everything from home.

The closer Bless got to their station he noticed the person that Ronda was laughing with and sharing information about the things that were on display. Immediately his heart sped up and his hands felt clammy. He had no clue why he was feeling the way that he was and he just hoped that God wouldn't strike him down because of it.

For a moment he just stood there admiring how effortlessly beautiful she was even in a simple outfit. She wore some distressed dark denim jeans that weren't too snug but fit just right along with a pair of Trin Sperry's that matched the Trin t-shirt that had her company logo on the back. That day she decided to braid her long thick hair into a simple halo braid that wrapped around her head. Anya was gorgeous and that was something that no one could deny.

"What's going on family?" Bless greeted them.

One would have missed the way that Anya's breath became labored like she was trying her best to control it upon hearing Bless' voice but Terrell and Ronda caught it. Giving one another a knowing look before responding to him.

"Hey bro," Ronda said coming around the table to give him a hug. His niece was so huge inside of her mother that she had to hug him from the side.

"I like her. That's the one," Ronda whispered before walking off as fast as she could. Well it was more of a waddle than anything.

"Good morning Bless," Anya smiled in his direction.

"Good morning baby, I mean um Anya," he replied getting tongue tied and making her blush. If Jesus was to come back in that very moment there was no doubt in his mind that he wouldn't make it in because of where his thoughts were. He had just called someone other than his wife baby. It was inappropriate but it felt so natural.

"Aye bro Mama said once you got here to come to her office. You in troubleee," Terrell laughed as he passed on the message that Bless' mother had given him.

"Let me go see what she wants then. I'll be right back," Bless told them but was looking right in Anya's face.

Speaking to a few people along the way he finally reached the church doors and headed inside to find his mother. He didn't know what she wanted but he had hoped she would tell him fast enough for him to be able to head back outside.

"Hey old la-," he started but was cut off because of the scene he had just walked into when he opened the door to his mother's office. "God gonna get yall trying to be fresh in His house."

His parents began to laugh being caught red handed in the middle of their kiss. They had been married for over 30 years and the love that they had for one another was still just as strong as it was in the beginning of their relationship. Maybe even stronger.

"Oh hush God knows what's up," his dad told him.

Pastor Matthew Williams was in his mid-fifties but didn't look a day over thirty. Often times when Bless was out with his dad people mistook them for brothers instead of father and son. They looked so much alike that it was scary. The only difference was that Bless had dreads and his father kept his curly mane cut low.

"That's right baby," his mother said before giving her husband another kiss just to mess with their son.

"Enough is enough. What was so important that I needed to see you?" he asked her.

His mother Geneva was a short little thing standing at only 5'5" with pretty chocolate skin and dark doe shaped eyes. She wore her hair in a stylish pixie cut and even had a little of it highlighted. First Lady Geneva Williams looked nothing like some of the pastor's wives that he had seen but that's exactly what made her stand out and people accept whatever it was that she spoke to them.

"Mandy brought the list of vendors to me and there's someone here that I think could help you with some property for your store. I haven't gone out to meet her yet but she's a real estate agent so you should see what she has to offer."

"You mean Anya?" Bless asked and couldn't help but to smile a goofy grin.

Geneva looked down on the sheet that she was given to see if that was the young lady's name and sure enough it was. Who was this woman and how in the world was she affecting her son the way that she was? If she wasn't eager to meet this Anya before she definitely was now.

"That's her. How do you know her?" his mother questioned him.

"Oh she comes into the store a lot. She's good people," he replied nonchalantly.

"Mmm hmm," was all she said as she watched him closely. There was definitely something in his eyes that she hadn't seen in such a long time and that was admiration.

"If she's making you act this way then I have definitely got to meet this girl," his father joined in.

"It's not like that we are just friends. Besides I'm married and you both know that I take my vows seriously."

"You're the only one that does," his mother mumbled underneath her breath but he had heard her just as clear as day.

It was no secret that his parents didn't really approve of Trinity but they were the type of parents that loved their child regardless of his mistakes and in their opinion his marriage to Trinity was a mistake.

"Is there anything that you all need my help with?" Bless asked trying to change the subject.

"Yeah come help me set up this bounce thing for the kids. I know they have been waiting to get on it," his dad told him.

While Bless walked off with his father to the area they needed to be in Geneva glanced at the list of vendors to see which booth Anya was at and made her way to the outside. Looking around at all of the smiling faces she was glad that God had placed her in the position that He had in order to help his people. With the jobs being a little slow and quite a few of their member jobless this was something that He had placed on her heart to do. She prayed that by the end of the event there would be no one left without being blessed in some way.

Finally, she spotted the direction that she needed to go in and moved swiftly. If the woman that she was looking at was indeed Anya then she could totally understand why her son was acting the way that he was. She was beautiful and was the complete opposite of Trinity and that was a good thing.

"Good morning my loves," Geneva greeted them.

"Hey mama," Terrell said before giving her a big hug. Even though she wasn't his real mother she had been in his life for practically all of his life and when his mother passed she made sure to be there for him.

"Hey son. Hey mama's baby and grandbaby," Geneva squealed as she rounded the table to wrap her arms around Ronda and rub her belly.

"Good morning ma. I sure do wish your grandbaby would come on out. I'm tired of being pregnant," Ronda informed her while shaking her head.

"In due time baby. You gotta let my princess come when she is good and ready. And who do we have here?" she asked turning her attention to Anya.

"Good morning ma'am I'm Anya," she greeted while trying to shake her hand.

Looking down at her hand like it was a foreign object and then back up to Anya, Geneva made a face that Anya couldn't read before she spoke.

"Oh no baby we don't do handshakes around here we hug. How are you darling?" she smiled causing Anya to release the breath she was holding and returned the smile.

The moment the two of them embraced there was a connection that they both felt. The presence of God was so thick and was wrapping itself around the two women and there was no way that it could be denied. It had been that way since Anya had pulled into the parking lot earlier. As soon as the tires on her car touched the pavement she knew immediately that she had just come upon holy ground and she basked in the feeling. From every person that she had come in contact with she felt more and more at home and at peace. But that wasn't what she was feeling. Anya wasn't sure of what it was. Geneva on the other hand knew right away but it wasn't the time to speak on it.

"I'm doing good how are you?" Anya asked politely.

"I'm blessed. Speaking of being blessed I've just learned that you are friends with my son Bless," Geneva spoke and waited. She wasn't really waiting on her response but more of her reaction at the mention of her son's name. Just as she had suspected the same sparkle that Geneva saw in Anya's eyes was the same one she had just seen a few minutes prior in her office.

Now Geneva would be the first one to say she believed in the sacred union of marriage and that anyone on the outside had no business stepping in where it didn't concern them. But she also believed that sometimes people married the wrong person. Not once did she get the vibe from Anya while standing there that she was trying to weasel her way into Bless' bed. She could tell that Anya was struggling with her feelings because she knew of his situation and Geneva couldn't do anything but respect that.

"Yes ma'am. I come into his store on the regular since it's between my house and my job," Anya explained.

Before either of them had the time to continue talking Bless and his father walked up to where they were standing. The moment Bless and Anya made eye contact Geneva saw right away the battle that was going on inside the both of them and she just prayed that God would do whatever it was that he was going to do. Just looking at the two of them all she saw was happiness and it was welcomed considering the fact that she knew the hell that her child was experiencing at home.

"So this is the lovely Anya. I'm the pastor here and this young man's father," Bless' father introduced himself considering everyone else was caught up in making wedding and baby shower plans for his son.

"It's nice to meet you Pastor," Anya replied.

"So I hear that you are a real estate agent," he continued.

"Yep one of the best," Bless jumped in once again causing everyone to look at him with amused expressions on their faces.

"Speaking of real estate, Bless the client that I sold

the house to yesterday said that he had some property that he was having trouble getting rid of. I told him to send the info and I would list it for him but the moment I saw what it was I decided to hold off on it," Anya told him as she reached for her phone. "Look."

Handing the phone over to Bless he took it from her perfectly manicured hand and looked down on the screen. The moment he saw it he understood what she was getting at.

"Aye bro that would be the perfect spot for your store. The building is already there and it's in a good neighborhood," Terrell said looking over his shoulder.

"That's exactly what I thought when I saw the pictures. Because it hasn't sold yet and he's tired of holding on to it he is willing to negotiate the price. I know this is something that you have wanted for so long and I think that it would be perfect," Anya beamed. She was praying that Bless wouldn't be too upset with her when she told him that she had scheduled a meeting with Mr. Dennis in three weeks when he returned from a business meeting out of town. The minute she had reached out to the owner of the house with the numbers he immediately responded with a yes. Since she was going to meet with him to sign the papers she thought it would be good for him to meet with Bless about the property.

"Man An you are full of beauty and surprises huh?" Bless said still admiring the different photos. He could already see how he wanted it set up and he couldn't wait.

"I just know how important this is to you and I wanted to help in any way that I could. Every time you talk about your own store I can see the excitement in your eyes. I hope you don't mind that I set up a meeting with you and Mr. Dennis when he returns to town in a few weeks to discuss it. He's closing on his house and needs to sign a few papers so I told him that we could possibly do everything at one time," Anya revealed before biting her bottom lip. Something that Bless noticed that she did when she was nervous. It was crazy to him how he had picked up on those little things by only talking to her at the store.

"Yo I don't even know what to say besides thank you Anya. Like for real you didn't have to go through all of this for me," Bless told her.

"I know but it's something that I believe in for you. I don't think God had us cross paths for no reason. He used me to be able to bless you," she told him genuinely.

"I know that's right," both Geneva and Ronda said at the same time. If anyone ever wondered how many teeth they had in their mouths they didn't have to wonder anymore. The big smiles that were stretched across his mother and his sister's faces showed them all.

"Um excuse me, I saw the sign about real estate and I was looking to get some information," an older woman interrupted them.

"Oh yes ma'am, I'm Anya how can I help you?" Anya greeted the woman before excusing herself and walking away to work her magic.

"Wow," Bless' father said in awe.

"What?" Bless asked.

Instead of him answering right away Matthew looked over to his wife and shook his head. He was a firm believer that God would never send anyone a spouse that belonged to someone else but he also believed that people sometimes moved too fast when it came to choosing a mate.

"Do you remember when I preached the sermon *Out of Order*?" Matthew asked his son.

"The one where you made reference to Jesus telling the Disciples which donkey to bring to Him?" Bless asked.

"That's the one. And what was the lesson in that?"

"That people are out of order when they tell God what it is that they are going to do or want when they need to be looking to Him for the direction. When we take it upon ourselves to move on something that isn't for us we mess up the order that He set for us."

The day that his father had broken down the scripture during his sermon was one that he would never forget. Out of all of the times that Bless had studied his word he had never understood it clearly until that day. Zachariah had already prophesied that Jesus would ride in on a donkey and for that prophesy to be fulfilled Jesus had to let them know which donkey was the one. The donkey they were to bring to Him was appointed for that time specifically for Him so he couldn't just choose any one. Nor could anyone bring to Him the donkey that they felt was the best. If they had they would have been out of order.

"You see son, God already knew who your wife was but you chose not to wait on her. I know that you may love Trinity but can you honestly say that you know without a doubt that she was who God sent to be your help meet?"

The more Bless thought about it the more he understood where his father was coming from. He couldn't say that God presented Trinity to him because if he did it would have been a lie. He had been so smitten with her as a young boy when she came along that he wasn't thinking clearly. She had a way to make him second guess what he knew was in his heart just to please her. But why hadn't God stopped him from making that mistake if it was indeed one?

"Free will baby boy," his mother said as if she was reading his mind. "God gives us free will to either follow Him or do what it is that we want to do. He's a gentleman and will not force anything on us because He knows that sooner or later our eyes will be opened to what it was that He was trying to get us to see. By then we either choose to surrender to His Holy will or continue to do our own thing. Keep your eyes open Bless and see things for what they really are. If Trinity was the type of woman and wife that was encouraging, loving, supportive and anything else that a wife should be but maybe had an issue in one area where she lacked, let's say in the bedroom, then I would tell you to fight for your wife. You would be surprised at how many couples we counsel in that one area of their marriage. Your situation is different though baby. The ass, I mean donkey, that you decided to pick wasn't the one that He had for you," Geneva told her son before walking away with her husband leaving him there to think about what she had just said.

Was it possible that Anya was who he was to be with and not Trinity? Looking over at her while she spoke with the people that approached her table he admired her beauty and how she interacted with them. Like she belonged there. Something that Trinity never did. Out of all of the time that they had been married he could count only a handful of times that she had actually gone to church with him and when she did she never spoke with anyone.

"All I can tell you to do bro is to pray about it. Ask God to reveal to you what it is that He wants you to do and when He gives you the answer don't challenge it this time. He doesn't need our help we need His," Terrell said patting him on the back and walking off to go and help one of the elders of the church.

Bless heard everything that everyone close to him was telling him but the last thing he wanted to do was disappoint God by making the mistake of letting his heart fall for the wrong woman. Or had he already done that when he fell for Trinity. He hadn't realized that he was still staring at Anya until she looked up at him and gave him a warm smile. The way his heart fluttered in that moment seemed to make his knees weak and he knew that if he didn't leave then he would be in trouble. Bless needed to get somewhere and pray so instead of returning the smile he abruptly walked off and headed inside to the sanctuary.

"Did I do something wrong?" Anya asked Ronda when she saw Bless turn and walk away.

"No boo he'll be alright. God is just revealing some things to him and he's not quite sure how to handle it," Ronda explained.

Anya knew exactly what she meant because the more that she was around Bless the more God was revealing things to her as well. As bad as she wanted to remain in her lane and not have her mind and heart attach to someone else's husband she was beginning to fail miserably and slip back into that place. Maybe it wasn't a good idea to be around Bless until she could clear her head. The last thing that she wanted to do was to make a move that could cost her to lift her eyes up in hell.

-7-

Trey Songz voice blasted through the speakers of Trinity's car as she made her way through the streets headed towards her man's house. *Disrespectful* could have been her theme song and by the way she was singing along to Mila J's part one would think that she had wrote it herself.

"I don't care about nobody but you. Boy you so special. I don't mind being disrespectful," she sang.

If someone would have told her years ago that she would be married and creeping with another man she would have told them they were absolutely right. Bless was never the man of her dreams but no one would ever know it except her parents. They knew her better than she knew herself sometimes and because of that they weren't blind to what she was doing. No matter how many times they tried to talk her out of it the harder she went to get him.

Trinity was full of greed and for the life of them her parents couldn't figure out where she had picked up that trait. They made sure to do their best by raising her up the way that God had instructed them to but she was hell bent on doing things her way. Driven by money and money only, was the reason that she was in a loveless marriage for almost a decade. Well her marriage wasn't completely void of love because Bless loved the ground that she walked on. The feeling just had never been mutual and she was ready to go.

As she drove through town she thought about the true love of her life and couldn't stop the smile from stretching across her face. Just the thought of Dre seemed to make everything in her world right and when they were together nothing else mattered. Especially not Bless. She tried to remember a time when she had loved Bless like she now loved Dre but it was never there. The yearning to see his face each day and to lay beside him each night was what she craved but not because of love. It was because of the future that she had predicted she would be living.

When Trinity met Bless they were in high school and he was every scout's dream player. She knew that with the skills that he possessed on the field he would be drafted to the NFL right out of high school. Although his parents were against it and wanted him to go and get his college education first, Trinity on the other hand tried her best to have him sign that contract so that she could live the life that she felt belonged to her. In the end he had listened to his parents and decided to go to college. It seemed that all hope wasn't lost though when he had made that decision because NFL teams wanted him even more because he was so focused. Bless was a star on the field and they wanted him no matter how long they had to wait.

Knowing that he would still get the chance to make her dreams come true Trinity got him to agree to marrying her by the end of their sophomore year at the University of Georgia. Surprisingly she didn't have to push him as hard as she had thought she would considering he was already head over heels in love with her. They didn't have the big wedding that she wanted because she didn't want either of their families to try and talk them out of it before she became Mrs. Bless Williams so they went to the courthouse instead. When they returned back home for the summer and announced their good news the looks of disappointment were evident on not just his parents faces but hers as well. She already knew that would be their reaction but she didn't care because she was about to live the life of a trophy wife. Or so she thought.

Two years after they had said their vows to one another her dream along with Bless' had flown out of the window in the blink of an eye. It was the last game of the season as well as his school career and the fourth quarter had just begun. Bless was the star quarterback and had been breaking most of his own records all night so his adrenaline was at an all-time high. There was only 43 seconds left and just as the ball was hiked for the life of him Bless couldn't find an opening to pass the ball. With none of his teammates in a good enough position to receive the ball he decided to run it himself. That one mistake changed his life forever.

Bless was less than three yards from the end zone when seemingly out of nowhere one of the players on the opposing team tackled him causing him to land on his left leg in an awkward way. The landing was so severe that his femur bone broke. It was so bad that a part of the bone could be seen poking out of his skin. Just the sight of it let everyone around him know that was the end for him. Now whenever he walked there was a slight limp that was a constant reminder to them of one of the worst times in their lives. Of course for different reasons.

The ringing of Trinity's phone took her away from her trip down memory lane as she looked at the display on her dash to see her mother calling. Groaning out loud she debated about whether she wanted to answer the call or not. Knowing Ernestine Jones the way that she did she knew that all her mother would do was hang up and call right back. Her best bet was to answer and get it over with so that she could enjoy the rest of her day.

"Hello Mommy dearest," Trinity said dryly.

"Well hello to you too my dear," Ernestine replied ignoring the tone of her daughter's voice. If they had been face to face Trinity would have been picking her lips up from the floor but since she wasn't in her presence she could live another day.

"How can I help you Mama?"

"For starters you can change that tone of your voice before I have you picking up your lips while standing outside the Pearly Gates. I don't know what crawled up your little scrawny behind today but don't play with me," her mother snapped.

Ernestine may have been an Evangelist but she didn't play when it came to the disrespect. She may not have cursed but the way she would read a person that got on her bad side would make you think that she did. Her mother was old school and no matter how old Trinity got she had no problem getting her right back in line when she thought she could try her.

"Now that we have that clear, what are you doing?" she inquired.

"Headed to the store why?" Trinity had an idea of why she was asking so she just waited for her mother to reveal it.

"And where is my wonderful son-in-law?"

There it was. She knew that it would only be a matter of time before Bless started contacting everyone that they knew to find out where she was. For some odd reason her parents were always on his side and would call her fussing like she wasn't their flesh and blood.

True enough she had been back in the city for a few days but no one needed to know that especially her husband. What he didn't know wouldn't hurt him so there was no reason to tell him her every move.

"In his skin," Trinity tried mumbling under her breath.

"Jessie!" Ernestine called out to her husband and Trinity's father. "I need you to send up a prayer to the Lord for your daughter. She's about to get that wig snatched off along with the little bit of edges she has left talking to me like she lost her mind. Little girl keep talking to me like you on drugs and watch me forget that I'm trying to make it into heaven. I may be saved but my drop kicking skills still on point. You know what? Wherever you are you need to contact your husband. He's been looking for you for two days and I know you ain't been on no flight this whole time," Ernestine went in on her.

"Mama now you know how hectic my schedule is and sometimes things change with flights."

"So just because things change with your job that means you don't have to call and check in with your husband?"

"Why is it that everyone is so *pressed* about me telling *my* husband where I am all of the time like he's my daddy?"

"When I see you I'm gonna *press* my *fist* against your *lips*. Keep on Trinity Diane! Getting my pressure up. I'm gonna say this and then I'm getting off so I can go into my prayer closet and repent for the beat down I want to give you. That ain't of God but He may have to close His eyes for a few. Anyway, I know in my spirit that something's not right so take heed to this warning. That grass that looks so much greener on the other side is always artificial," and with that Ernestine ended the call. She was so heated that she didn't even bother to tell Trinity goodbye not that it mattered one way or another as long as she was off of her phone.

Throwing her phone into the cup holder and unbothered she made her way to her destination. Just as she was pulling up to Dre's house her phone rang again and this time it was Bless. Trinity parked the car and looked up at the house to make sure that Dre wasn't coming out to greet her like he normally did before answering.

"What Bless? I'm about to board the plane," Trinity lied. Unbeknownst to her Bless knew that she was lying this time unlike all of the other times but he wasn't about to call her out on it. If it wasn't for him being on 3-way when her mother called her he would have probably believed her.

"Baby it's been days since I've talked to you and I was getting worried. Now that I know you're alright I can rest a little easier. What time do you get in?" he asked.

"Tomorrow afternoon and then I have to leave out again on Friday." The lies she told were flowing out of her mouth like a waterfall and not once did she feel even a twinge of guilt.

"They giving you overtime or something. You never just have one day off between flights especially when you've been gone for some time," Bless acknowledge. He knew pretty much how her schedule went so all of this extra stuff she was doing was out of the norm. Still he chose not to say a word. He was just glad to hear her voice and know that she was ok.

"Listen," she began as she looked up at the house again. This time she saw Dre peep out of the window and she knew that it would only be a matter of seconds before he came out to assist her so Bless better make it quick.

"What did you need Bless I have to board now."

"I wanted to tell you that I think I found the perfect property for my store and get to meet with the owner on Thursday. I was hoping you would be here to go with me to meet with the guy and see it," Bless told her with his voice filled with excitement.

"Boy bye. For one I keep telling you that little dream of yours is dumb and for two, in order to buy something that would mean that you have the money for it and we both know that's not true. Your account tells it all boo. Anyway, I gotta go." This time it was her that had ended a call without saying goodbye just as Dre walked outside.

"Hey baby. I got everything that I needed to cook you that amazing meal that you wanted," she told him as she got out of the car and walked to the trunk to grab the bags. She was about to make him her special lasagna that he loved so much.

Instead of him responding to her he watched her intently before asking his next question. Trinity was sneaky and he knew that but she had a way of never letting anyone see her sweat when she was caught up.

"Who were you just on the phone with?" Dre asked her.

"Nobody but mama begging me to come to church Sunday but I let her know that I was working. Bae can you grab these last two bags please?" she asked as she tried to walk around his big frame.

When he reached his hands out Trinity just knew that he was about to offer her some assistance but that didn't happen. Before she could do anything about it Dre had snatched her phone from her hand and went to her call history. Now any other person would have panicked but not her. Trinity was always ten steps ahead of the game so she was as cool as a cucumber. Being that Dre had never met her parents for obvious reasons she knew that he wouldn't recognize any of the numbers in her phone.

Trinity watched as Dre scrolled through her phone and she was pretty sure that he saw the last number that called was listed as *Mommy*. Satisfied that he didn't find anything out of the way Dre handed her back her phone causing her to smile inwardly. Before he allowed her to go around him he eased up on her invading her personal space and leaned his head down. His lips were so close to her ear that his breath caused her to shudder with excitement. That was until he spoke.

"The moment I find out that you have been doing something that you had no business will be the moment your family starts selecting pictures for the front of your obituary."

The breath that Trinity was about to take immediately got caught in her throat. Did the man that she was in love with just threaten her? Never had Dre done or said anything that would make her think that he had a violent side so she decided to blow it off. He had been ripping and running lately for work so she knew that he was tired. Instead of getting angry or letting fear consume her she got her mind prepared to feed her man good and give him the kind of loving that would have him relaxed and sleeping like a baby. Everything and everyone else was put on the backburner when it came to him and she was going to make sure that he had no reason to question her love or loyalty ever again.

-8-

"God I can't wait until I have this baby," Ronda said as she rubbed her perfectly manicured hand across her protruding belly.

"Don't worry it will be any day now that you'll be holding and smelling that beautiful little doll of yours," Anya told her as she turned her head away and wiped away the tear that was threatening to fall.

After the event at the church she and Ronda had been inseparable. The whole day they had been laughing and talking like they were the best of friends and not once did Ronda make her feel like she was being fake. A vibe that Cassidy had been giving her for the longest. She may have been her best friend but that was sadly because she was her only friend. Since moving back Anya didn't do a lot of the things that she used to do so that meant that the women that she used to be around were no longer there. That didn't bother her most days but now that she was back around Bless and the feelings she tried to hide were starting to resurface, she needed someone that she could confide in. Ronda was that one.

"You alright boo?" Ronda asked picking up her glass of iced tea from the table. They were sitting inside of Red Lobster feeding one of her many cravings.

Usually Terrell was available to pick those things up for her but since he was over at the church helping out for a few hours she decided not to bother him and ask Anya to accompany her. There was something that Ronda just loved about Anya besides the fact that she was one of the sweetest women that she had ever met. The moment she was introduced at the church event she knew they would be good friends and so far that had been proven. They had grown so close in such a short time that they didn't go a day without talking.

"I'm fine," Anya replied trying her best to plaster a smile on her face but Ronda wasn't buying it.

"See now we haven't lied to one another so don't start now. What's wrong hun?" Ronda asked calling her out.

Sighing Anya debated within herself if she wanted to share that part of her life that she had closed off with anyone. She knew that if she didn't get her thoughts out they would eat away at her and cause her to shut down completely. That dark place that she was familiar with wasn't one that she wanted to return to so she decided to confess.

"This stays between us alright?" Anya said immediately getting a side eye from Ronda.

"Now I know we haven't been besties long but I do think that you know how I am by now. But if I must say it, you don't have to worry about that. As long as you aren't in any danger of hurting yourself or anyone hurting you then I'm good. So spill it missy," Ronda told her honestly giving her signature smile.

"I was pregnant once and lost my baby."

"Oh my God no! I'm so sorry An. How long ago was this?"

"Right before I moved back here. That was actually the reason I came back. My fiancé at the time was very abusive and didn't want children. When I found out that I was pregnant I was going to leave so that I could have my baby in peace because I knew that if I stayed and he found out he would make me have an abortion. That was not happening. My baby may not have had a father who loved them but they would never have to question the love from their mother.

Well before I had the chance to get everything together to leave town I was outed," Anya explained.

"What do you mean you were outed?" Ronda asked confused.

"Come to find out that one of Nardo's side chicks was in the office the day that I found out and because she knew about me she ran back and told him. By the time I got home he was there waiting for me. I did my best to act normal but the way he was acting had me nervous and he picked up on it. He grabbed my purse out of my hands and found the ultrasounds and prenatal vitamins. It felt like he beat me for hours before I woke up in the hospital to doctors and nurses giving me their condolences for my loss."

"I'm so sorry sis. I can't imagine how difficult that must have been for you. Did he go to jail?" Ronda wanted to know as they both sat with tears rolling down their faces.

"No," Anya confessed as she shook her head and wiped her eyes. "I knew that if I told on him I wouldn't live to see another day but God still answers prayers. I ran and after I got back here I found out that he got locked up for attempted murder on the same girl that had snitched on me. She was so close to death that the state decided to press charges on him. From what I learned it was so severe that he got sentenced to twenty five to life."

"That's good for his ass," Ronda said shocking Anya.

"Did you just cuss?" Anya laughed?

"I shole did. I have a reserved bank full of cuss words that I have permission to use when the time calls for it and that was one of those times. Now I have to go another month without using one before I can recoup that one," she laughed.

"Girl you are crazy." Anya felt so much better sharing that part of her life and she knew that it was the start of her complete healing process.

"Do you still want children?" Ronda asked.

"Absolutely. I dream of the days where I hear the little feet running around the house and calling out to me or my husband. Just thinking about it makes my heart swell with pride."

"You sound like Bless. He can't wait to have a house full of babies."

It was as if the mention of Bless' name made her remember there was something else that she had to reveal.

"There's something else that I need to tell you but I want you to know that I never planned this."

"Okaaay," Ronda said with an eyebrow raised.

"I've been in love with Bless since I was in the ninth grade."

"What?!" Ronda almost yelled before she remembered they were in a public place.

"We met online when we were in high school and," Anya began but was cut off.

"And one day the communication just stopped," Ronda finished shocking Anya to her core.

"H-how did you know that?"

"Excuse me," Ronda called out to their waitress instead of answering Anya's question.

"Yes ma'am," their waitress said walking over to them.

"Can we get the check please?"

"Sure I have it right here."

Anya sat there watching what was going on around her but her thoughts were going a mile a minute. How was it that Ronda knew what she was going to say? Had Bless mentioned her? No he couldn't have because they were so young and it was only an innocent friendship. Or was it? She was so far into her thoughts that she hadn't even noticed when Ronda was done paying and was grabbing her by her arm.

It took them a minute to get to Anya's car because of Ronda wobbling and dealing with a few Braxton Hick's but they had finally made it. The moment their doors were closed Anya went in.

"How did you know what I was going to say? I swear I didn't come here to start any trouble in his marriage. Does he know who I really am? Oh my God this looks so bad. I know I shouldn't have said anything," Anya panicked.

"Calm down girl dang," Ronda tried her best to laugh through the pain that was hitting her lower back.

"Are you alright?"

"Yeah it's just a little Braxton Hick's contractions but I'm fine. But no Bless doesn't know who you are. Shoot I didn't even know until you said that you met him in ninth grade and as soon as you said that it clicked. I have heard so much about the girl that first had Bless' heart and how he always wondered where you disappeared to. One day he was preparing to beg his parents to bring him to wherever you were and the next you had disappeared and he never heard from you again. He searched for your profile but could never find you," Ronda revealed. By the look on Anya's face she could tell that something wasn't right. "What's wrong? Why you looking like that?"

"What do you mean that he looked for me? I was the one that was looking for him but could never find him again. I didn't have any other way to contact him because we hadn't exchanged numbers but I never stopped talking to him. Bless stopped talking to me. Once I came back and ran into him at the store and saw he was married I didn't bother telling him who I was. There was no need to because the last thing I wanted to do was to break up a happy home."

"Psst happy? Girl bye but anyway something doesn't sound right. If you are saying that he stopped talking to you but he said that you stopped talking to him something isn't adding up." Ronda thought as they drove back in the direction towards her house. Just as they were about to get to the exit she was hit with a sharp pain followed by a big gush of water.

"Ohhhhh God!" she yelled out in pain.

"Did your water just break?" Anya squealed out in a mixture of excitement and panic.

The only response that Ronda could give was a frantic nod of her head as she concentrated on the breathing techniques that she had learned in her Lamaze classes. Never in her life had she felt anything like she was experiencing and never again did she want to ever feel it. It felt like her soul was being ripped out through her lower body and God was showing no mercy. It made her try to remember a time that she had sinned so bad to cause this much pain.

"Hey Terrell, it's Anya. I'm on my way to the hospital with Ronda her water just broke," Anya told Terrell as Ronda noticed that she had taken her phone and made the call for her.

"No we were at lunch and on our way back to the

house when it happened," she said and paused to hear him speak.

"No she didn't have anything spicy. Huh? Boy how am I supposed to know that? She doesn't know either Terrell. If you don't calm down and get to this hospital! You can find out all of that and more. We are pulling up now," Anya laughed before hanging up in his ear.

"What he say?" Ronda inquired through breaths.

"Your husband is so special. Why did that man as me how many centimeters dilated you were like we would know," she laughed.

"Lord have mercy I know this baby better hurry up before her daddy runs all of these people off with all of his questions."

"He can't help it. He's excited and I could hear it all in his voice."

"Well he better enjoy this one because as bad as I'm hurting there won't be any more popped out of here," Ronda sassed with much attitude as Anya helped her from the car to the awaiting wheelchair. It was time to welcome one of her biggest blessings into the world and no matter how much pain she felt she couldn't help but to thank God in that moment.

-9-

"She's so beautiful bro," Bless said as he looked down into his niece's face and admired her. He couldn't help but to think about what it would be like when he was finally able to hold his own child in his arms. The love he had for this little girl was nothing compared to what he could and would give to his son or daughter.

"She really is. Have you all come up with a name for her yet?" Anya asked standing beside Bless and using her index finger to gently rub the baby's exposed arm.

To say that watching Ronda give birth was one of the most touching experiences she has ever witnessed would have been an understatement. She was shocked once Terrell had arrived that she was asked to stay in the room to witness along with Bless. Ronda and Terrell both agreed that they wanted the two people who meant the most to them to share in this blessing with them. Anya may have been new to the group but she had fallen right into step with them.

"They look good together don't they?" Terrell whispered into his wife's ear.

The two of them admired the way that Bless and

Anya looked so comfortable around each other and how the chemistry they tried to hide was in plain view. Ronda understood the dilemma they were facing but from where she stood she had to give them credit where credit was due. Neither of them made any move towards the other and respected the sanctity of marriage. Something that not too many people these days did.

So many times women and men knew that someone was married and still moved forward with being in an outside relationship. Never having respect for themselves or the spouse. It was all about what they could get out of the deal and no one else mattered. That was until the other spouse found out and all hell broke loose. By then it's too late and the damage is already done.

"They sure do," Ronda replied slipping out of her thoughts.

"You pick out your matron of honor dress yet?" he teased causing her to laugh a little louder than she had intended drawing attention from Bless and Anya.

"What you two over there sniggling about?" Bless asked with his killer smile on display.

Anya tried her best not to look at him and those dimples but she was failing miserably. Something about those pearly white teeth and his boyish but manly features did something to her heart and those old feelings were beginning to become even harder to suppress.

"Oh nothing," Ronda giggled.

"Mmm hmmm keep on that's how you got this one here," Bless joked.

"And it's gonna be how you and Anya get one too," Terrell mumbled through unmoving lips and only loud enough for Ronda to hear. "Ouch!" he yelped the minute Ronda elbowed him in his side.

"I heard you nut," she smiled and looked back over at her baby girl. "We decided to name her after her Godmother."

"What?" Bless asked shocked. He knew that he was automatically the baby's Godfather but he had no idea that they were going to name her after Trinity. It was clear to everyone that knew them that neither Ronda or Terrell were very fond of his wife.

"We just thought that it would be best," Terrell said with an unreadable look on his face.

"So she's gonna be named *Trinity*?" Bless asked just to be sure.

"Oh hell no! You know I don't like that wanch. My baby will not be named after that edgeless bat," Ronda expressed while rolling her eyes for that full effect of her being disgusted.

"Aye! Watch yo' mouth girl. No more cussing," Terrell scolded his wife.

"Keep on and you are never going to recoup that word bank of curse words," Anya laughed.

"See you know me so well already," Ronda laughed.

"Her name is Anya Leone but that's only if you accept the position as her Godmother," Terrell revealed.

"Wha-who? Me?" Anya asked shocked with tears coming to her eyes. Never had she imagined that she would be given the honor of being this little beauty's God mother let alone have her named after her. It was so overwhelming she couldn't stop the tears from falling.

"Man how y'all gonna make my girl cry like this?" Bless asked as he placed his free arm around her shoulder and pulled her close. He may not have realized what he had just called Anya but everyone else in the room did.

The minute Anya was pulled close she couldn't help but to smell the scent that permeated from Bless' skin. It was so intoxicating that she couldn't help but to inhale deeply and melt into his arms. The connection that was between them was so strong that it caused Bless to be momentarily caught up in the moment. It was a feeling that sadly he had never felt with Trinity.

Time stood still as Ronda and Terrell watched

something powerful take place until the sound of a phone ringing brought them out of it.

"Oh that's my phone," Anya nearly yelled while cursing herself internally for getting so close to Bless but it felt so right when she knew that it wasn't.

"Ok then sis! So you bad and bougie huh?" Ronda asked referring to the Migos ringtone that was coming through the phone as she got hype in the bed.

That she is, Bless thought to himself.

"Chiiiiile," Ronda exaggerated hearing Bless speak what he clearly thought he had said to himself.

"Umm, I'll be right back," Anya hurriedly spoke before answering her call and closing the door behind her.

"Bro you got it bad," Terrell expressed while shaking his head.

Bless couldn't deny his friend was telling the truth no matter how much he tried and wanted to deny it. There was just something about Anya and he didn't know what it was. It wasn't just him wanting a fling because she possessed everything that Trinity didn't, there was something deep there. Like if he wasn't married to his current wife he could definitely see himself being in a committed and loving relationship with Anya.

"God forgive me," Bless said somberly just as Anya walked back into the room.

"Hey Bless that was Mr. Dennis that called. He said that his schedule has changed a bit and that if he couldn't meet today then he wouldn't be able to for another month or so. He and his fiancé are going on a pre-baby vacation. You think you can make it? I have all of the paperwork ready if so," Anya said biting her lip again. Bless found that to be one of the cutest things she did.

"Um absolutely. I just don't have my car. When you called Terrell earlier we were together and didn't have time to drop me back off," Bless explained while he handed baby Anya to her mother.

"That's fine I don't mind driving and the café he wants to meet at isn't far from here," Anya said grabbing her purse.

"We'll let's do it."

"Good luck bro. I know God got you covered in His favor so this is already yours," Terrell encouraged before giving Bless pound.

"To God be the glory," Bless responded before heading to the door.

"I'll call you later," Anya told Ronda before giving her a quick hug.

"Tell him," Ronda said only loud enough for the two of them to hear.

"I will but not now."

Not bothering to say anything else Ronda nodded her head because she trusted that Anya would reveal her secret to Bless in due time. The last thing that she wanted to do was pressure her and cause her to close herself off. She just prayed that Bless didn't get upset that Anya had held the information from him for so long.

-10-

The whole way to the café Bless prayed that God worked everything out in his favor. He had wanted to be a business owner for so long and he could feel it within his reach. There was no way that God had brought him this far just to leave him. Looking over at Anya as she drove he noticed how deep in thought she was about something. He didn't know if it was about the deal that she was about to make on his behalf or if it was something else. Whatever it was it had to be serious.

"Aye you ok An?" Bless asked her.

"Huh? Oh yeah I'm fine. Just getting in my zone for this meeting. I really want you to be able to land this deal," she told him somewhat truthfully.

Anya definitely wanted him to be able to purchase the building for his store but that wasn't the only thing on her mind. She was in a battle with telling him who she really was and wondering how he would take it. Would he be mad at her and think that she was stalking him? Or would he be glad to finally have her back in his life? If it was the latter how would that affect his marriage. There was no way that she was about to be playing second to any woman and she knew that how you got a man sometimes was the same way that you would lose him. That was one thing that wasn't on her agenda. Living in a life of adultery wasn't part of her plan.

"So if you're fine why did you just past the café?"

"Oh dang!" Anya yelled out as Bless laughed while she made an illegal U-turn in the middle of the road and found a parking spot across from where they needed to be.

"Calm down An. If it's in God's will it will work out in our favor. If not then He has something better in store," Bless encouraged the both of them.

Smiling Anya gathered her things that she would need and got out of the car. Bless had already given her all of his bank records, credit reports, and anything else she requested that would help him land this spot. From where she was looking he was a shoe in for this but it was all up to Mr. Dennis and if he wanted to accept the offer. She had prayed diligently about this situation and she had a pretty good feeling that God would open this door for Bless.

"Good afternoon, how many?" the hostess greeted them.

"Oh we are meeting someone here and I see him in

the back. Is it alright if we go on back?" Anya asked once she noticed her client sitting alone in the back.

"Sure go right ahead. I think your server was waiting for you to arrive," the young girl stated with a bright smile.

"Thank you," Anya said leading the way. "Hi Mr. Dennis."

"Anya. What did I tell you about calling me by my father's name?" he asked standing to his feet.

"I know, I know but I always do my best to remain professional."

"I understand. You must be the man of the hour? I've heard nothing but great things about you. I'm Emmanuel but everyone calls me Dre," Mr. Dennis turned his attention and hand towards Bless.

Sticking his own hand out to shake the man's in front of him, Bless greeted him, "The pleasure is all mine. I appreciate you taking the time to meet with me."

"I'm glad to be finally getting rid of this property. I couldn't understand why it wouldn't sell but now I see that God must have been waiting on the right person to send my way."

"You have no idea how long I have been wanting to have my own store. I know that it will eventually open up other opportunities to bring jobs back to our people in the neighborhoods and hopefully one day I will have more than one," Bless expressed with a wide smile on his face.

Just watching him talk about his dream of helping others while being a provider for his family did something to Anya's heart. The more she listened to the interaction the more she fell for the man that sat beside her.

"Well I'm glad that it will go to someone that will do good with it. I don't want to seem like I'm rushing you all but once my fiancé comes out of the bathroom we are heading to Aruba for three months. She's almost three months pregnant and I want to spend a little alone time with her before the baby comes," Mr. Dennis told them.

"No problem. I have to make it home before my wife anyway. If everything works out I want to surprise her with dinner before I give her the good news," Bless told him immediately regretting doing so. The way he felt Anya tense up beside him made him feel some type of way but he wasn't sure why. It wasn't like she didn't know that he was married and he had never given her any impression that his home wasn't completely happy so why was he feeling like he had just hurt her?

"Ok so I have everything ready to sign for both the

house and the store property. If the numbers are good then you both can sign on the document above your names," Anya hurriedly spoke. For some reason she felt like she was about to cry and didn't need anyone to see it. She just didn't understand why Bless' comment hit her so deep.

"No need. I went over everything already. I have the keys here and I will go ahead and sign both," Mr. Dennis said while he passed the keys to a smiling Bless and took the pen that Anya had extended to him. Once he was done he slid everything to Bless to do the same. The moment it was signed all hell broke loose.

"Sorry it took me so long Dre but this baby of yours has me going through-," Trinity spoke but immediately stopped when she looked up to see who her fiancé was sitting with.

"My little man is a handful already huh? Anya our realtor and Bless this is my fiancé Trinity. Baby this is the man that just bought the store that we had been holding on to forever."

"Oh really? Congratulations, Bless is it?" Trinity fronted like she didn't know who he was.

"Ain't this some bu-," Anya started only to be cut off by Bless.

"Really? So you gonna just stand here and

continue to pretend?" he asked her with eyes full of rage and pain.

"Excuse me?" Trinity asked like she was really confused.

"What's going on here?" Dre asked. He could feel the anger that he tried to keep boxed up inside of him about to be exposed.

Neither Bless or Trinity spoke as they were both caught up in their own thoughts. She was wondering how she was going to explain all of this to Dre and keep living the secret life that was finally out in the open. Bless on the other hand was feeling a pain so deep like nothing he had ever experienced in his life. To see his wife standing in front of him with a man that referred to her as his fiancé carrying the baby that he had always wanted caused him to feel like his heart was being ripped from his chest.

"Ok let me say this," Anya began.

"You shouldn't be saying anything. Why are you here with my husband?" Trinity blurted out.

"Husband?!" Dre yelled causing everyone in the room to look in their direction.

"Like I was saying before I was rudely interrupted, the business we have just completed is legal and binding and does not relate to this personal matter. So Bless congratulations on being a business owner and thank you Mr. Dennis for this awesome commission but that has nothing to do with the fact that this trifling heffa is about to get dragged," Anya spoke way too calmly as she put the papers securely in her briefcase and began to kick her heels off.

If it wasn't for Bless grabbing Anya around her waist and Trinity jumping behind Dre the café would have been a WWE event. Tables and chairs would be all over the place with Anya's fist down that woman's throat.

"No An she's…pregnant," Bless choked out. Just the sound of his voice and the pain that he was experiencing caused Anya to forget about her own feelings and focus on him. But that was short lived.

"You protecting this homewrecker? That's alright you can finally have him. Isn't that why you came back anyway *Manae*?" Trinity blurted out.

"Manae?" Bless asked stepping away and releasing her body like she was a ball of fire.

"It's not what you think Bless," Anya tried explaining.

"Yes the hell it is. My cousin told me you came back to try and break us up because you were mad about him dropping you the way that he did." She lied.

There was no way that she was going to own up to all of this by herself. The moment that Anya had told Trinity's cousin Cassy about her past and the man that she was in love with who still had her heart, Cassy couldn't wait to run back and tell it. They had both been scheming even in high school about how to land a baller by any means necessary. Cassidy stole hers just like Trinity had stolen Bless from the one girl that he truly loved. Instead of Trinity taking heed to the warnings about Anya she pushed Bless further away and now lives were torn apart at the seams.

"But guess what boo," she continued, "it wasn't him that disappeared it was me who blocked the two of you to make it look like the other just all of a sudden stopped talking. I wasn't about to let him make it to the pros and I not be the one on his arm. Only he failed at that like he failed at everything else. So you can have him. I need to focus on my fiancé and our baby. I'll have my lawyer deliver the divorce papers since they have already been drawn up for a while now and you can be on your way."

And with that Trinity turned on her heels, grabbed a mute Dre's hand, and left both Anya and Bless standing there in their thoughts.

"Bless," Anya said barely above a whisper after a few minutes of silence. Every pair of eyes in the place were still glued to them but he was numb as she tried to reach out to him. Instead of responding to her or even looking in her direction, he just shook his head and slowly moved out of her reach towards the front door. Leaving Anya there with a heavy heart and a face full of tears.

-11-

Trinity watched as Dre got into the car without one word to her. Any other woman in her position probably would have felt bad because of the things that took place but not her. She was actually relieved that everything was finally out in the open so that she could move on with her life. A life that she was dedicated to building with Dre.

When she met Dre on a flight to Amsterdam almost three years ago she knew from the moment their eyes met that he was the one for her. Besides him being one of the finest men on the face of the earth he was paid out the behind. It wasn't a secret who he was because he was well known. So when he asked her out while they were both out of the country she jumped at the chance to be with him.

The whole three days that she was there they were inseparable. From him showing her the finer things in life, also known as spending uncounted amounts of money on her, she knew that with Dre was where she wanted to be. He was able to afford her the life that she should have been getting from her husband and the sex was off the charts! Dre may not have been as gentle and attentive to her needs as Bless was but as long as he was satisfied that was all that mattered to her. His happiness trumped hers every day of the week.

"Is that my baby?" she heard Dre ask with an even tone. She couldn't make out what exactly he was thinking or feeling because he was unreadable.

"What? I know you didn't just try and play me like that," Trinity huffed.

Dre didn't bother to say one word. All he did was chuckle lightly as he drove down the highway towards their house. He couldn't believe that Trinity had been married the whole time they had been in a relationship. For her to be able to keep that big of a secret he wasn't sure if there was anything else that she was hiding. Trinity played the part of a doting girlfriend and that was the reason that he had proposed in the first place. Seeing as how she had made a fool out him he would spend the rest of his life making one out of her.

Pulling up to the house they both got out of the car and headed towards the steps before Dre stopped her by pulling gently on her arm.

"I'm sorry baby. I know that the baby is mine. It's just a shock that you're married that's all," he told her softly while looking into her eyes.

"I'm sorry that I didn't tell you in the beginning but that marriage had run its course long ago and I was so unhappy. I just didn't want you to back away knowing my situation. But I promise that you don't have to worry about me going back to him. I had papers already drawn up for a divorce but didn't get around to having him served yet," she explained.

"How do you feel about getting married as soon as the divorce is final. We can do something quick and then once the baby gets here then we can have that big wedding you always wanted."

The smile across her face let Dre know that he had her right where he wanted her and that she was about to ride with him until the wheels fell off. Knowing that they didn't have much time before they needed to get to the airport, he pulled her in closer to him and kissed her sensually. For some reason his kiss didn't feel the same and Trinity couldn't place it. Maybe it was just because of everything that just happened. Whatever it was she knew that it would be fine eventually. Breaking their kiss Dre took her hand and led them to the house to make sure they had what they needed for their trip. In Trinity's mind she was about to have the time of her life but thoughts of pure evil was taking over Dre's. This would definitely be the last get away that she would be taking because she wasn't about to get away from the wrath that was brewing inside of her soon to be husband.

-12-

Fourteen Years Ago

"Girl you'd be stupid as I don't know what to let another girl get Bless before he makes it to the big time!" Cassidy told her cousin.

Trinity and Cassidy were sitting up in her room going through Bless' chat account. He had no idea that she had hacked into his personal messages to see what she could find out. For the last few months she had been noticing a change in his behavior whenever they had a been at school to the point where he was starting to ignore her. Granted he wasn't her official boyfriend but they were almost there in her mind.

When Trinity started seeing how big of an impact he was making on the field and people were starting to take notice early, she knew that she had to lock him down but she didn't think that she would have to move that fast to do it. She felt like her subtle flirting and banging body would be enough to draw him in but now Cassidy had confirmed that she needed to move a lot faster.

"Please believe this right here is the end and I'm

gonna be the one on top. He doesn't even know what she looks like so there is no way that he could want anything serious with her," Trinity said confidently although on the inside she was second guessing herself.

No way could this Manae person look better than her or do the things that Trinity could. And on top of that she didn't even live close to him. Long distance relationships never worked out and with him always practicing and school there would be no real time for the two of them. Online or otherwise. She was about to make sure of it.

"So what are you going to do?" Cassidy asked excitedly while leaning off the side of the bed. She didn't want to miss a thing. Mess and gossip was something that Cass loved to be in. Nothing else gave her more joy than knowing someone else's business.

Before Trinity could respond her bedroom door opened with her mother standing on the other side with a scowl on her face.

"What are y'all doing in here?" Ernestine asked with a raised eyebrow. It was no secret that when her daughter and her niece got together they were bound to be in some trouble and Ernestine hated it.

There was no way that she would say that she didn't love her daughter and niece but she couldn't stand their ways. They were two of the most selfish girls that she had ever met and offered no apologies for their behavior.

"Nothing auntie I'm just helping Trin with her homework," Cassidy lied. Ernestine knew darn well that it was a lie because although her niece was beautiful she hated to say that she was as dumb as a bag of rocks. Just no common sense that the good Lord gave her and her grades were even worse.

"Mmm hmm well hurry up because we have Bible study tonight," she told them before backing out of the room. Ernestine knew that they were up to something and in due time it would be revealed. For the life of her and her husband they couldn't figure out how to get and keep their baby girl on the right track. She was so defiant that it was insane.

"Was that the only lie that you could come up with?" Trinity laughed.

"What you mean?"

"Cass come on now. You know good and well if anyone was getting help with homework it would be you and not me."

"You ain't cute hussy. Anyway, so what are you going to do about Bless?"

"Well for starters I'm going to block her. That way he can't find her and she can't find him," she explained.

"Why not just cuss her out in a message and be done with it?"

"Because don't you think he can see that when he logs in on his computer? I know she will respond and that will send up a red flag to him that someone was in his account. Plus if he's upset about her not talking to him and he can't find her anymore, then that's where I can come in as the shoulder to lean on. Before you know it I will be the only girl on his mind. If I'm down for him before he makes it big he will have no choice but to think I'm loyal to him and I will have a bank account full of commas and zeros!" Trinity said excitedly before slapping five with her cousin.

There was no way that her plan would fail and she would do anything that she had to in order to secure her future as a football wife. If she had to pretend to be in love with someone that she knew she would never love just to get to the money he was sure to have then she would do it come hell or high water.

It had been close to six months since Trinity had caused the so called breakup between Bless and his online love interest. He had been moping around once it happened and she was right there to be the ear that he needed to vent to. Before long the two of them were inseparable and everyone around them hated it.

If it wasn't Terrell and his friends telling him that

he needed to be careful with her then it was the both of their parents. She heard on the regular from her mother how she felt that Bless wasn't the one for her but there was nothing that anyone could have done about it. Just like she knew it would happen, Bless had fallen head over heels for her and the last chick that he thought he loved was a thing of the past.

To people that didn't know Trinity she played her part very well and would swear on their life that she was the doting girlfriend and would make a wonderful wife. They just didn't know how selfish she really was. It even amazed her that Bless never picked up on it but she did have a way with him that no one else had. Trinity had no idea that one decision to change the direction of their relationship would end up causing not just Bless a world of hurt but her as well.

-13-

"He still not answering?" Ronda asked Terrell as she fed her daughter. They had been home from the hospital for two days and had yet to hear from either Bless or Anya. No one knew if the deal was complete or not and neither were answering their phones.

"Nah. Let me try mama," he told her before placing a call to Bless' mother.

"Hey my big baby! How's nana's baby girl doing?" Geneva asked once she picked up the phone.

"She's good ma. Taking this milk like a champ," Terrell beamed as he admired his baby girl. She was the prettiest baby that he had ever seen. Cheeks as she was affectionately called because of her huge chubby cheeks was the spitting image of her mother. With her soft caramel complexion, dark brown eyes, and full lips she was Ronda reincarnated. The only thing that she had from him was his soft, incredibly thick, and curly hair. Ronda was in for it when baby girl got older and it came time to doing her hair. She was adamant that he would be learning how to do some hair but he didn't know if he was anointed for that.

"I can't wait to get back into town and see her. I hate that we missed her birth."

"I know ma but she will be right here when you and pops get back waiting on you to love all on her."

"So what's going on? Everything alright?" she wanted to know. Although Terrell sounded joyful there was still a twinge of something else in his voice that concerned her.

"That's what I'm trying to figure out. Bless left the hospital the other day and was supposed to be going to meet with the guy about the property with Anya but I haven't heard from him since. Ronda tried calling Anya but she wasn't answering either. I been so busy with making sure Ron and the baby were situated and haven't gotten the chance to go by and check on him."

"Hold on a sec. Matt!" she yelled out to her husband. They were about to head out to the last day of the Holy Convocation they were attending in Orlando but if something was wrong with her baby boy they were about to be a no show and head home.

"Yeah baby?" Matthew asked her as he stuck his head out of the bathroom door. He was doing his best to get his tie just the way he wanted but for some reason it just wasn't working.

"Have you talked to Bless?"

"Not since we left. Why?" he asked with concern etched across his face.

"Terrell can't reach him or Anya and they left the hospital the other day together. I'm worried," she replied already getting in her mind that she needed to change their flight and head back home. Something in her told her something wasn't right and rarely was she wrong when it came to her intuition.

"Let me try calling," Matthew said walking over to the dresser to retrieve his phone. He knew his wife very well and if she wasn't settled in her spirit about something she wouldn't be able to function until the issue was resolved. If they were going to minister to God's people at the service he needed her head clear so that she would be able to hear from God. Right now he knew her mind was a cluttered mess especially when it came down to their son.

"Matt is calling him now," she told Terrell on the other end.

They waited for what seemed like forever when it was actually only a couple of seconds. The first time he called the phone rang twice before going to voicemail and when he hung up and called right back it went directly to his messages.

"He's not answering. It's going straight to voicemail."

"Rell baby hang up so I can call and change our flight out. Something isn't right and I need to get there.

Oh God let my baby be alright," she rushed off the phone while Matthew began to throw their things in their suitcases. He had to make sure that he called the presiding Bishop and let him know what was going on and apologize for the inconvenience.

"They haven't talked to him either. You gonna be alright until I get back? I need to go check on him?" he said before getting up and reaching for his shirt that was on the back of the chaise in their bedroom just as the doorbell rang.

Ronda got up from her spot in the rocking chair and walked down the stairs behind Terrell with the baby in her arms. Before they could reach the door good, whoever was on the other side was very impatient and began beating on the door and hitting the bell simultaneously.

"What in the world?" Terrell said to no one in particular as he snatched open the front door to find a heavy breathing, tear stained face having Anya standing on the porch.

"Oh my God Anya!" Ronda exclaimed almost knocking her husband out of the way trying to reach her friend.

Anya stood there shaking like a leaf and looking like she had been in a fight with a wild animal and lost. Her hair was all over her head and she had bags under her puffy red eyes. She never really wore much makeup and was naturally beautiful but this look wasn't normal.

"Sis what's going on?" Terrell asked placing an arm around her shoulder and ushering her into the house.

"Have you talked to him?" was all that she said looking like she was in a daze.

"Talked to who? What happened?" Ronda wanted to know.

"He knows and I know that he hates me now. It's all her fault!" Anya yelled scaring the baby and causing her to yell out in distress.

"Let me go put her down baby and you talk to Anya," Terrell advised her before taking his daughter carefully and cradling her. Instantly making her relax and within seconds she was asleep again.

"What are you talking about Anya? What's going on?"

Taking a deep breath Anya recapped everything that happened when they left the hospital and got to the meeting all the way up until Bless walked out on her without a word. She had been trying since then to reach him but by now he had blocked her. Not knowing where he lived didn't allow her the option to stop by and make sure he was alright.

"*You*?" Terrell asked in shock once it was revea-ed that she was indeed the girl that Bless had fallen in love with all those years ago.

He knew that there was something about her when he met her that afternoon at the store but never in a million years would he have thought that she was the girl from ninth grade. This was crazy!

"So Trinity really was on some bu-," Ronda started only to be cut off by her husband

"You better not cuss," he told her sternly. She was getting carried away with her curse word bank as she called it. She had to have been negative by now because she had been swearing like a champ.

"I just want to make sure he's alright. I know he may be mad at me for not telling him but I promise I was going to eventually. After talking to Ronda I knew that I needed to let him know but I never expected things to play out the way they did."

"Wait a minute Ronda you knew?"

"Don't be mad at her she just found out the day she went into labor. She had no clue," Anya defended.

"Why didn't you tell me?" Terrell asked. It wasn't like he was mad but he wanted to sip the tea too and Ronda was holding out on him.

"Um you try pushing a whole human out of a hole the size of a golf ball and tell me if you want to talk about anything else besides some potent pain meds. Besides we didn't have a chance to get deep into the conversation before your baby decided to come."

"Yall I'm sorry for everything and I don't mean to sound rude but can y'all do this later? I just want to make sure Bless is alright and I can rest knowing that he's fine," Anya interrupted.

"You're right sis. Our bad. Rell was just about to head over there to see if he's there. You can stay here with me if you want," Ronda spoke as she hugged her friend.

"Do you mind if I go with you? I mean I just have to see his face even if he's mad at me," Anya pleaded.

"Nah let's go," Terrell agreed before kissing Ronda and grabbing his keys.

The whole way to Bless' house Anya did something that Terrell had never witnessed Trinity do and that was pray for Bless. The prayer that she prayed aloud was so powerful he almost had to pull over and gather himself.

"God I don't know what is going on but I do know that this is your will. Please keep Bless covered in the blood and protect his heart and his mind. Let him know that greater is coming and that he already has the victory. Lord I thank you for his life, in Jesus' mighty name I pray, Amen," she concluded just as they pulled into his driveway.

Noticing that Bless' car wasn't in the driveway Terrell didn't know if he was home or not. He had no idea if he had even gone to the church and picked it up or not considering that the last time they were together they were in Terrell's car before going to the hospital. Still he had to check just in case. Nothing looked out of place and it was eerily quiet.

Knocking once he placed his ear to the door and waited to see if he could hear any movement. After a few more seconds he knocked again and listened once more. Hearing a car door close behind him he turned around to see Anya out of the car and walking towards him with her arms stretched high above her head and was once again praying. She was a winner and once Bless got himself together he would be wise to go ahead and wife her. If she was back in his life after these years then it was a reason that God had brought her back.

Returning his attention to the house he still didn't hear anything. Not even the TV was on and that was strange. For some reason Bless would always have the TV on even if he wasn't watching it. He just liked to have some type of noise since most of the time he was always home alone.

"Do you have a key?" Anya asked breaking his concentration. He didn't know why he was still standing outside when he did in fact have one.

"Man I don't know why I didn't think of that," he chuckled as he shook his head and reached inside of his pocket.

Once the lock clicked Terrell took a deep breath and opened the door slowly. Easing inside the house nothing looked out of place from where he stood.

"I'll-," he started but stopped abruptly when Anya bumped into him almost losing her balance.

"Oops my bad," she said embarrassed. She was so into looking around that she wasn't paying attention to where she was going when Terrell stopped walking.

"You good. I'll go check upstairs and you check around here," he instructed before taking the steps upstairs two at a time.

Anya could hear him moving about above her but she was stuck in place. She didn't know if she should be snooping around Bless' home without his permission. In her mind she wasn't one of his favorite people at the moment so how would that look if he came in and caught her going through his things? But on the other hand if something was seriously wrong and there was a clue that could help her and Terrell find him then she needed to find it.

Pushing her first thoughts out of her mind she went from the hall bathroom to the kitchen and back to the living room. Still no sign of Bless or Trinity for that matter. Not that she expected to find Trinity there after what happened at the café. Just the thought of that day and the pain that Bless felt made her eyes begin to water before she noticed something on the table beside the dark brown and cream sectional by the window. Walking over to it and reaching for the papers Anya studied the letter and realized that she was looking at divorce papers that held both Trinity and Bless' signatures. His divorce was final.

"Dang she wasted no time did she?" she said to herself.

"Nah she didn't," Bless said from behind her causing her heart to leap from her chest and scurry right out of the front door.

"Oh my God Bless!" she nearly shouted as she took in his appearance.

Gone was the man that she always saw so put together even in his work uniform. Now a man that she almost didn't recognize stood before her with his hair needing a severe wash and retwist. The clothes that he wore the last time she saw him were still on his soiled body and the stench that permeated from across the room was not his signature cologne. It smelled more like old sweaty socks mixed with a little must and a whole lot of liquor.

Anya didn't know if she should stay where she was and explain what she was doing in his house or run to him and wrap her arms around his neck because he was alright. Slowly she moved towards him with a look of empathy on her face. Bless looked so broken and all she wanted to do was take his pain away.

"Don't," he said halting her in her tracks and stabbing her in her heart. Her worst fear seemed like it was coming true and that was the main thing that she had wanted to avoid once she had found her way back into his life.

The fear that she had that he would hate her was starting to become very real but there was still a part of her that hoped she was wrong.

"Aye bro! Where the hell you been? Got everybody worrying about you," Terrell fussed as he flew down the stairs. One look at his best friend and he already knew what time it was. The smell of Cîroc and weed was evident and it pained him to watch.

Bless ignored the both of them as he turned on his heels and walked back in the direction in which he had come. It was a miracle that he didn't fall down the steps as he plopped down on the couch. The moment Terrell and Anya hit the bottom step they both covered their noses to block out the strong smell that almost knocked them out.

"Dang bro what died down here?" Terrell asked him seriously covering his nose as he spoke.

"My spirit," Bless said somberly with a shrug of his shoulders.

Terrell could hear the sharp breath that Anya took in and looked over at her. The tears falling down her face let him know that if he thought her feelings before now were fake, then the pain he saw her going through at that moment said they were genuine. He knew that when his brother got himself together and could focus clearly that Bless would see in Anya what everyone else did.

Before any of them could speak again Terrell's phone vibrated in his pocket. Seeing that it was Ronda he excused himself to go take the call privately leaving Anya alone with the only man who held her heart. Even if he didn't know that he possessed it. Looking around the room she saw that it wasn't as messy as it smelled. The dark cherry wood table that sat in front of the fluffy chocolate brown sofa was void of anything except two *Xbox One* controllers and a few coasters. Other than that the room was pretty spotless. That let Anya know that it wasn't the room smelling that way but Bless. Upon that revelation Anya also noticed that Bless was wearing the same clothes that he had on the last time she saw him. The day both of their worlds seems to stand still.

Turning around without a word she made her way back up the steps and ran right into Terrell coming back to the basement.

"What happened?" he asked with a concerned look on his face.

"Oh nothing. I was about to go run him some water so that he can get a shower and changed while I make him something to eat. I know he may not feel like it but he can't stay like this."

It took everything in Terrell not to let the huge smile he felt rising up and threatening to spread across his face come out. On the inside he was doing the Tootsie Roll because his boy finally had a winner in spite of the negative circumstances that caused them to come back together. This was where she was supposed to be and he was going to make sure that God's will would be done.

"Cool. Cool. Ronda needs me for a few so you think that you can stay here for a while until I get back? When I can break away I'll come back and pick you up so that you can get your car," he told her. The last thing he wanted her to think was that he was pawning his best friend off on her but Ronda and the baby needed him right then and he felt safe that Anya could be what Bless needed right then more than he could anyway.

"That's fine. I don't mind. Besides this will give me a chance to straighten up around here and get him straight hopefully," she told him looking around the room wondering where to start.

"Aiight, I'll be back as soon as I can and if you need me just call either me or Ronda," Terrell said as she nodded her head.

The moment the door closed she locked it and turned on her heels to head in the kitchen. She was going to start preparing his meal before she made him get in the shower. That way once he was finished he could sit right down to a hot meal and then relax on a full stomach. She knew that he hadn't eaten and he couldn't go another day without doing so. There was a small Bluetooth radio on the counter so she paired her phone with it and turned on Pandora. Her favorite station was VEDO's and as soon as his voice filled the air she instantly felt relaxed. She loved her gospel music but right now she just wanted to vibe out and get in her cooking element. Once she had the Rosemary chicken in the oven, the yellow rice, and French style green beans with diced potatoes on she made her way upstairs.

Stopping just at the second floor landing she thought about if she should reconsider her plan of starting Bless some bath water. Though he needed a good wash up and from the papers that were downstairs he was officially divorced, it still felt funny because this was the same house that he had shared with his wife. The last thing she wanted to do was make either of them uncomfortable. Battling with herself for a few moments she decided to go ahead with her plan. It wasn't like she was trying to be the woman in his life after this bad break up but she was definitely going to be the friend that he needed her to be.

It took her a minute to find the master bedroom but when she did it caused her to gasp. Stuff was thrown everywhere. The king-sized bed was a mess and there were pieces of glass that were broken on the floor that looked like they used to belong to a lamp that was strewn across the other side of the room. She could tell that either Trinity had come to retrieve her belongings or Bless had already gotten rid of them because nothing in the room even hinted that a woman had been there. That gave her somewhat a sense of peace to know that she wouldn't be touching another woman's belongings. Whether they were together or not it wouldn't have felt right. Trinity may not have respected anyone but Anya was a different breed of woman.

Forty minutes later the room looked a little bit better even though she wasn't done yet. The dirty clothes that she had picked up still had to be washed and put away, the bed had to be remade, and the floor vacuumed. She would worry about those details later. Right then she needed to get the water started and put him some clothes out to dress in before going back down to the kitchen. The food had to be done by then and he needed something hot on his stomach.

Finding his Axe body gel she turned the water on in the tub and poured a little of his wash in to make some nice bubbles. The scent that the gel mixed with the hot water did something to her senses and caused her to bask in its comfort for longer than she had planned.

"That chicken was on point," Bless said behind her causing Anya to almost jump out of her skin.

Grabbing her chest she dropped the bottle that was in her hand and closed her eyes praying that her heart would stop beating so hard. If it didn't she was sure she was about to meet her maker.

"Jesus Bless you scared the crap out of me," Anya finally got out once her breathing returned back to normal.

"What are you doing?" He asked watching her with a look on his face that she couldn't quite figure out.

"Um, well, I-I saw how everything was and how you were looking and thought that you might need a good meal and a bath. Maybe even a retwist of your locks," she said avoiding his eyes. The look was too intense for her and for the first time ever Anya was a ball of nerves around him.

"Hmph," was his reply as he closed in the space between them.

Anya bent over to turn the steaming water off before it over flowed and just as she came up she bumped into Bless. The electricity that she felt when their bodies collided clouded her thoughts as Bless turned her around and stared into her eyes. Without a single word he wrapped his strong hand around the back of her neck and pulled her into him, locking his lips with hers. Fireworks, a drumline, and violins all sounded off in Anya's head as he deepened the kiss. Just as she was about to slip into even more unchartered territory her senses kicked in and the taste of some type of alcohol and what she remembered as weed, filled her mouth. Pulling away and backing up a few paces, she watched a devilish grin spread across his face as he watched her intently before taking off his shirt.

Oh God in heaven! She thought to herself. No matter how saved and filled with the Holy Ghost she was, there was no way that Anya could deny one of God's greatest creations standing before her. The way his skin looked to flow over his body like warm melted chocolate had her unable to tear her eyes away from the sight before her. That was until the doorbell rang. Anya tore her eyes away from him and rushed out of the room so fast that she could have won an Olympic medal.

Flying down the stairs to the front door on wobbly

knees she swiftly opened the door to find Bless' parents standing there. In that moment she felt two inches tall just knowing that they were privy to what had just happened in their son's bathroom. If her shifty eyes weren't an indication of something going on, then her shaky voice would surely tell it.

"He-hey Pas…um Pastor and First Lady. How are you?" she sputtered out like an old hooptie backfiring.

The raised eyebrows they were both sporting made her feel like she was caught when she hadn't even done anything. It wasn't like she came onto him in his vulnerable state he kissed her first. She was just trying to help and be a good friend. There was no way that she would take advantage of him in such a way. So many thoughts were going through her mind and trying to come up with a logical explanation for his parents that she missed the knowing smiles that they were both wearing.

"How is he?" his mother asked. It took everything in her not to break out into a shout by seeing Anya there at the house. They were both so worried about their baby boy all the way home but once they heard from Terrell on their way over and he let them know that Anya was there with him, they were able to somewhat relax. Yet they still didn't have the full story on what was really going on. Terrell felt that it was best if Bless told them. But there was no doubt in both Matthew and Geneva's minds that he was in good hands but they at least wanted to see him with their own eyes first. That was the reason that they had rung the bell instead of using their key to gain entrance into his house. If Anya was there they knew that Bless was good.

"Well I got him to eat something and I ran him a bath so that he could relax. I was just finishing cleaning up and about to do his laundry before I called Terrell to come get me and take me to my car," Anya explained. The looks of approval that flashed across his parents faces calmed her nerves a little and she was finally able to relax. But only a little bit. Part of her felt like they knew that something had gone on between her and Bless and she didn't want them thinking anything bad about her.

"You are just the total package huh," Matthew said more to himself than to her.

"I was just raised to be this way. Nothing special," she said averting her eyes around the room. Just the thought of her parents made her want to cry but she had to keep her tears at bay.

Anya was one of the lucky kids in the foster system to be placed in a home with two loving foster parents who really wanted her to feel love. It wasn't that she wasn't loved by her biological parents, it was just that they weren't able to let their life before they had children fully go once she was born.

Anthony and Tanya, hence the name that she was given, both had a rough life growing up. Parents who were addicted to drugs and alcohol raised them up in a lifestyle that trickled down to them. They became a product of their environment so to speak. Anya's father became heavy in the dope game and her mother was right beside him holding him down. Neither of them ever wanted to bring a child into the world under those circumstances like their parents did them but eventually Tanya got pregnant with their only child. It was like the minute that they found out they were expecting their views changed. Just not fast enough.

When Anya was just three years old one decision that her father had made cost him their lives. Anthony had in his mind that he could hit just one more big lick before he was out of the game for good and that was just what happened. Somewhere some money came up short and the men that her father had made the transaction with came right to their home. No words were exchanged as guns were blazing through their spacious three-bedroom home. If it wasn't for Tanya diving on Anya the moment that she did, all three of them would have lost their lives that day. Because her life was spared and there was no other living family that could take her she was placed into the system.

It took no time for her to be placed with Reginald and Janie Mae O'Day. The two of them had wanted children of their own for so long but sadly they were never able to conceive. Being that they were both spiritual and trusted God with their whole hearts they knew that it was His will for them to become parents in another way. For almost twenty years they were foster parents to thirty children over the years but none of them pulled at their hearts the way that Anya had when they set their eyes on her. From the moment when they saw the beautiful little chocolate doll they knew that she was sent to them straight from God. It took a while but they finally were able to adopt her two years later on her fifth birthday.

The life that Anya was provided by them all the way up until they passed when she was twenty was one of perfection to her. They showed her unconditional love through not only their words but their daily actions. She was raised up in church but it wasn't forceful. It was used as a tool to guide her but not to where she grew tired of it. Often times church became too much for some because of the way that *tradition* was taught instead of the importance of having a relationship with God was. Tradition didn't allow God to flow freely and confined Him to a box when He was so much more than that.

Never once did her adoptive parents keep her mother and father a secret from her. They did all they could to find out as much information about and pictures of them as they could so that she would always remember them. When she was old enough to understand what happened to them was when the revelation was revealed but it was done in such a way that she loved them even more for at least trying to give her a good life. She was thankful that God loved her so much that he had given her two sets of parents to instill characteristics in her that she would be able to teach her children one day. That's if she ever was given the opportunity.

Anya didn't realize that she had been so zoned out and taken back down memory lane with a simple comment from Matthew until she felt the arms of Bless' mother embracing her. That was when she realized that the tears that she tried so hard to hold in had finally made their escape.

"Don't cry sweetie. Bless is a strong man and he will be just fine," Geneva told her warmly. They thought she was crying for their son when they had no idea that she was really crying to be loved again. Something inside of her though gave her comfort in knowing that soon she would receive the answer to her prayers.

"You go ahead and do what you were going to do and let us run and check on Bless, ok?" his father said to her.

There was something about the young lady in front of him that spoke volumes to him and his wife and he hoped that one day his son would be able to pick upon that. But only when his heart was ready. There was no mistaken the fact that his son loved his wife even if she was no good for him. That's just the type of man they had raised. All Bless ever saw was how his father loved his mother and he craved for that relationship. Only he craved it so much that it had blinded him from the truth that was staring him in his face. Trinity was only out for self.

"Yes sir," Anya replied while giving a soft smile and wiping her face before walking off down the hall towards the laundry room. The comfort she felt in that moment was enough to give her the much-needed strength that she needed to put her feeling to the side for now and focus on making sure that Bless was going to be alright.

***

Neither Matthew or Geneva knew what they were about to walk in on when they had made their way upstairs. They had an idea that something was wrong but no clue to what it was that had caused Bless to fall off the grid. Slowly they opened the door to his bedroom and immediately Geneva knew something was off.

"Oh Lord," she said barely above a whisper. She had been at his house and in his room more than once and just by looking around the clutter free space she noticed not a trace of Trinity was in the room.

"What?" Matthew asked trying to figure out what was going on.

"Look."

"Look at what?" he asked confused. He was looking around trying to see what his wife was seeing and nothing stood out to him.

"Lord you don't never pay attention to anything," she said shaking her head. Matthew rarely paid attention to the simplest details but Geneva did. Often times he had told her that she needed to work for the CIA because of how she investigated and caught on to everything.

Just as he was about to say something smart his

eyes landed on the papers that lay on top of the dresser.

"Wow," was all that he could manage to get out while he read the signed divorce papers.

"What?" Geneva asked walking over to him and peered over his arm. Being that she was so much shorter than him she had to stand on her tippy toes to read because of how high up he was holding the papers.

Noticing how bad she was struggling to see he passed it off to her and waited for the explosion to come. He knew his wife better than she knew herself and her reaction was one that he was prepared for. Silently he watched her face go through a series of emotions. Confusion was first because she was trying to figure out just what it was that she was reading. Then came the recognition of exactly what it was. Finally, fury showed up and it was on!

"I know that bald eagle, gorilla feet having, no good hussy did not do this to my baby! Wait 'til I see that little heffa. All of these years she didn't catch these hands because I loved my son enough not to go there but this is the last straw. Why would she do this to him knowing how much he loves her and wants this marriage?" Geneva went off just as the bathroom door opened and Bless walked out still in the same clothes that he had on when Anya left him.

"Because she's engaged and pregnant with another

man's baby," he said with his words laced with defeat.

"WHAT?!" his parents yelled at the same time.

"Son what are you talking 'bout?" Matthew wanted to know. There was no way that Trinity could have possibly stooped that low even if she was as low down as they came.

Bless sat on the side of his bed and took a deep breath before letting his parents in on everything that happened. By the time he was done they both stood in front of him speechless which was rare for his mother. Geneva always had something to say.

"It was Anya," Bless continued.

"What was Anya?" his father wanted to know.

"Remember when I was in high school and I would spend all those hours on the computer?"

"Boy running up my AOL account. How could we forget? Then you had the nerve to try and get us to take you to meet some girl. Hadn't even talked to her on the phone but wanted us to gas up the Pacer."

"Ma we didn't have a Pacer," Bless laughed for the first time in what felt like forever.

"Well you know what I meant."

Geneva watched too many old episodes of *Martin* he thought.

As soon as the laughter ended his previous words had finally registered in her brain. Geneva's mouth dropped to the floor as she understood what Bless was trying to tell them.

"Well I'll be a monkey's uncle. God and His strategic plans."

"Yeah well I wish that God had told me that Trinity had planned all of this so that I could avoid the heartbreak," Bless told them before standing up. His drunken stupor and the high that he was previously feeling was beginning to come down and he needed to shower.

"Son you know God always has His reasons of why He does things and we don't always understand or agree, but it's necessary. We just have to trust Him. How do you feel knowing that Anya is now back in your life?"

Shrugging his shoulders, Bless took his left hand and rubbed it down his face before he answered honestly.

"Pop I'm still in shock. When Trinity blurted it out at the café that day I didn't respond very well and I left Anya just standing there. I know she was hurt but I just didn't know what to do at that moment. So many emotions ran through my mind and I couldn't process it fully. Like after all of these years the girl that I fell in love with and gave my heart to is the same one that I thought broke my heart. Now she's back and for the last five years we have been almost like the best of friends. She knew who I was but I was left in the dark. How fair is that?"

"Baby it's very fair. Anya made the choice to not complicate things for you. As much as you were already dealing with when it came to Trinity and your marriage do you really think that you could have handled it back then? You have to remember that she too thought you had abandoned her so take a minute to think about how she felt. I can look at that girl and tell that she still loves you, so walking into that store to see you and find out that you were married could have caused her to be bitter. Anya could have caused a scene but she didn't because she put your feelings before her own. She didn't want to open that door because unlike that slufooted gutter snake you married, Anya actually respects marriage."

"Lord have mercy. Neva baby, a slufooted gutter snake? Son go shower so I can take your mother to the church and lay her at the altar. She's cutting up and I need God to lay hands on her," Matthew said shaking his head and holding back his laughter.

It was no secret that neither of them cared for Trinity too much but Geneva couldn't stand her the most. From the time Trinity was introduced to them she made it clear that girl vexed her spirit. She only dealt with her on the strength of Bless but now that it was over it felt like dead weight had been removed from their family. Now he could heal and move on with someone that would treat him like the king that he was.

"I don't know what to do with these feelings that I'm having. I know that there is no way that I would go back to Trinity after this and I can't say that I don't love her because my feeling were real. It's just that Anya…" he trailed off.

"I get it Bless. We understand because we know the kind of man we raised. Of course your love was real for Trinity but your feelings for Anya were real too."

"They still are real and that's what's scaring me."

"As much as I want to tell you to go downstairs and tell my daughter-in-law how much you love her I know that isn't the thing to do," his mother said.

"It may be true but to her she's gonna feel like you are just saying that because of a rebound thing. That could damage whatever you may try and build together and that's the last thing that either of you want. Pray about everything and seek God on what to do. If you leave it up to your mother y'all will be married tomorrow," his father jumped in.

"Shole God will," Geneva confirmed with a big smile on her face.

"Once you pray and get your answer then you do whatever it is that He instructed. If you get the green light, like I know you will, start courting her. You never had the chance to do that with Trinity because she wasn't into that kind of stuff. All that was on her mind was getting you because she had a vision of being a trophy wife but now you have a chance to do it right with the right one."

"I hear you Pops. I appreciate you and ma for everything," Bless said before hugging both of his parents. They prayed over him before telling them that they loved him and would check on him later. Leaving him to his shower and the many thoughts that were going through his head.

-14-

Two hours after Geneva and Matthew had calmed down and gone home, Anya had Bless' house completely spotless and smelling good, the food was put away, and she was folding up the last of his clothes when he emerged from upstairs looking refreshed. The way her heart fluttered when their eyes connected almost swept her from her feet but she could still see the sadness in his eyes. Turning away she decided not to say anything until he did considering that she still didn't know how he was dealing with the information about who she really was. She knew that shouldn't take priority of his feelings but she couldn't help but wonder what was going through his mind and if she was on it.

Folding the last shirt and placing it neatly on his coffee table along with the other articles of clothing Anya took a deep breath and finally spoke.

"Um I was just about to call Terrell to come and pick me up. In case you get hungry the food is in the oven," she told him reaching for her phone.

"I 'preciate it," was all that he said.

Not sure of what to do next she gave him a tight lipped uncertain smile before she went to her call log to place the call. Right before she hit the green call button he spoke again.

"Before you go can you help a brother out with his hair?" he asked her.

Nodding her head she finally noticed that he was holding his hair products in his hands as he made his way to her. With each step he took Anya felt like her breathing was becoming more and more choppy until it caught up in her throat when he sat on the floor by her legs. She felt light headed and had no idea why this man had her reacting to him the way that she was and she had to find a way to stop it. But how?

Slowly she sat back on the couch and sat where he could sit comfortably between her legs as he passed her the things she would need. It had been so long since he had gotten his dreads twisted and he knew that she would be spending a few hours on it. Just what he wanted or better yet what he needed. Bless had been in the house alone for far too long and he felt like the walls were slowly closing in around him. That was until Terrell showed up with Anya in tow. The moment he saw her he wanted to take her into his arms but he didn't know if he was really thinking clearly. It wasn't possible for him to forget Trinity so fast even if she had forgotten him long ago. Just thinking about how everything played out was about to send him into that dark pit once again.

"Let me know if I hurt you," he heard Anya say

softly.

No one could hurt him any more than he already was but instead of telling her that he just nodded. The gentleness of her fingers massaging his scalp with the coconut oil before she began twisting caused him to slightly lean his head back onto her lap with his eyes closed. Seeing that he was totally relaxed and the tension that was visible in his body moments prior was gone Anya began to relax herself.

It was so quiet in the living room that all could be heard was the two of them breathing and unbeknownst to the other is was killing them both softly. Reaching for the remote in order to have the TV drown out their thoughts, Bless turned to every channel there was before deciding on one of the stations that played music. As soon as he stopped and the song played the both of them were faced with their past.

"I wanna love you, every night, every day. You know I need you in my life won't you stay," Donell Jones sang. This was the one song that they both said reminded them of each other when they were younger so they had officially claimed it as *their* song.

The elephant that was in the room was so big but they each chose to ignore it. Right then wasn't the time to discuss it especially with Bless' emotions focused on more than one thing. Not only had he found out that his wife had been cheating on him, but she was also pregnant by the other man, his first love had reappeared after years of being MIA, and he was now divorced all in the span of a week. Nothing was making sense and he was so confused. Where had he gone wrong in life and why was it him that had to go through it? Bless had been so stuck in his thoughts trying to figure everything out that he didn't realize how much time had passed before Anya tapped him on his shoulder to let him know that she was done.

"Dang I zoned out huh?"

"Yea," she laughed lightly.

"What time is it?"

"Oh shoot it's almost midnight," she said with alarm in her voice. There was no way that she was about to call and disturb Ronda and Terrell and asking him to come and get her.

"Really? It felt like only a few hours that you've been here. Or maybe my mind was just boggled down with stuff. I don't know," Bless spoke not really knowing what he wanted to say. He was just saying anything that would keep her talking back to him instead of her leaving. With everything going on in his mind he wanted, no he needed her to stay.

"I know. I guess I better call a cab or something to

take me to go get my car so I can head home," she said right before stifling a yawn. She was emotionally and physically drained. She too had had a rough few days and all she wanted to do was shower and rest.

"No you don't have to do that. I mean it's late and you shouldn't be out alone like this. Um, you can stay in the guest room I don't mind," Bless told her praying on the inside that she would take him up on his offer.

"I don't want to impose any more than I already have. I mean this is still the home that you shared with your wife and even though she has been disrespectful on so many different levels I don't want to be," Anya told him truthfully although she wasn't sure that she wanted to leave him just yet either.

"An stay. It's not like we are going to be sleeping in the same bed or even in the same room."

But babyyyy if we did! The little devil on her shoulder tried to hype her up.

Get thee behind me Satan! Her angel scolded on the other side of her. The two of them went back in forth battling over the decision that she needed to make but stopped abruptly the second Bless invaded her space. Her judgement was so clouded that she didn't even realize that he was just moving closer to grab one of his t-shirts along with a towel and rag from the pile of clothes that sat on the table for her.

"Here. I'm sure you know where the bathroom is and the room is just on the other side of it. It's the least I can do for all that you have done for me."

"Thank you Bless but you don't owe me anything. I did it because I wanted to not because I wanted something out of it."

"I know and that's what makes me appreciate it the most. I'm also sorry about earlier," he said referring to the kiss that he had given her while he was inebriated. The intense look that he was giving her was like he was looking deep into her soul.

Chiiile you can do it again if you want to!

Shut up!

The battle between good and evil had begun yet again in her head but she forced her lips to say, "You don't have to apologize. I understand and no harm done."

There really hadn't been any harm done she thought as she grabbed her purse from the couch and stepped around him. But there had definitely been something that was ignited in her and she just prayed that God would tell her how to deal with it. Because if she left it up to the good and evil that fought in her head she didn't know how strong she could be fighting that kind of temptation knowing that the man who held her heart was just in the next room.

"Jesus be a fence," she mumbled as she shut the bathroom door behind her.

-15-

The ringing of Anya's phone removed her from the deep slumber that she was in. She hadn't realized how tired she was until after she had showered the night before. As soon as her head hit the pillow she was out like a light. Anya had fallen asleep so fast that she didn't have time to even twist her hair after she had washed it so it was sitting on top of her head and not in a cute and stylish way.

"Hello?" she croaked out.

"Eewww did you brush your teeth yet?" Ronda giggled on the other end with her face balled up like she could smell her breath.

"Whatever. My breath stays poppin'," Anya sassed.

"Well you need to pop some toothpaste and Listerine in that mouth and get on up. Rell is about to bring your car to your house in a few after he stops by to check on B."

Anya got quiet on the other end and Ronda wasn't sure if she had fallen back asleep on her or not so she called out to her.

"An! You better not have gone back to sleep on me," she fussed.

"I'm not sleep," Anya confirmed before biting her lip.

"So why you get quiet when I mention Bless?" she asked smiling and paused until a thought hit her. "Oh I get it. You want Terrell to come get you first so you can go check on your boo with him?"

"First of all, he is not my boo," Anya started.

"Not yet," Ronda cut her off just as the baby started wiggling in her bassinet next to the bed.

"And second of all," Anya continued while ignoring Ronda's comment. "I'm still at Bless' house. She braced herself the moment the last word slipped from her mouth.

"What?!" Ronda yelled scaring baby Anya causing her to scream out in a high pitched screech.

"Baby you ok? What's wrong?" Ronda heard Terrell yell from downstairs before the thunderous sounds of his feet hitting the steps taking them two at a time. Just as he reached the room that she was in he noticed her cradling his baby girl doing her best to calm her.

"I startled her when I got a little loud on the phone.

I didn't mean to scare you too," Ronda expressed as she patted her little princess on the back soothing her instantly.

"Give me my baby before I push you on the floor," he laughed reaching for her tiny body.

"You hear that sis? Now that this little munchkin is here it's forget me," Ronda said faking like she was hurt with a pout on her face and everything.

"Girl bye, you would probably push him right on back," Anya laughed on her end. She loved the playfulness of their marriage. Although she had been around them only a short while she admired their relationship and prayed that one day she would have one that others would feel the same about. Sure they had their issues here and there but their love definitely outweighed them.

"That Anya? Tell her I'm bout to leave now and will be there shortly," Terrell relayed once again like he hadn't told Ronda that a little while before.

"Well you only need to make one stop cause she still at Bless' house," Ronda teased. She was so extra that Anya could hear the smile in her voice as she bounced on the bed and stuck out her tongue. She was a mess.

The look on Terrell's face was one of utter shock mixed with a whole lot of excitement. He knew it was too soon for Bless to get into a new relationship since the ink hadn't dried on his divorce papers yet but in his mind Anya had him first. He knew that if it was in God's will then they would unite as a couple. If not they would at least make great friends to one another.

"Oh word?" he asked.

Instead of responding Ronda listened as Anya let her know that once she got changed and showered that she would be over to check on them before hanging up. It was time for her to get herself together and leave before she crossed a line prematurely.

Bacon and eggs filled the air making her very aware of the fact that she hadn't really eaten in days. The way her stomach growled sounded like a lion cub was inside of her chasing a gazelle and that was not cute. Getting up she made her way to the bathroom with her clothes in hand. She hated that she didn't have a fresh change of clothes but considering she had no plans of a sleepover, there was nothing that she could do about it.

"Good morning," she said walking into the kitchen. She was thankful that Bless had sat out fresh toiletries for her so that she could brush her teeth and wash her face. Ronda was right when she said her breath was popping and not in a good way. Anya would have been so ashamed if Bless had smelled her breath.

"Hey An. You hungry?" Bless shot over his

shoulder before returning his attention back to the stove.

Out of all of the things that Bless was good at cooking wasn't one of them. He had gotten up early to try and surprise Anya with breakfast to thank her for everything but the way the eggs were quickly turning black to match the bacon he had almost burned, they may have to find another option.

"Bless what's that smell?" she asked. It only took a few short seconds for her question to be answered once she noticed the smoke.

Quickly moving towards him Anya noticed that he had the heat up way too high and was about to burn everything close to him down.

"Lord Bless the heat is too high!"

The smoke alarm sounded letting them know that there was no hope for the eggs and either they would try again or go out for breakfast. Being that neither of them had their car Anya decided that she would stand in the gap for their rumbling stomachs and make something edible.

"I was just trying to do something nice since you helped me out that's all."

"I appreciate that but I did it because I wanted to and not because I expected something in return."

Saying no more, Bless watched her move around the kitchen like it was hers and began to dispose of the burnt food and prepare something else. The way she did it effortlessly made him think if that was her rightful place. There, in his home, with him. He knew that they still needed to have a talk but he wasn't sure how to start the conversation. Was he supposed to just come right out and ask her why she had never told him who she was or did he ease his way into it? And what about that kiss? He knew that he had drunk way too much and even went back to an old habit that he had years ago but that still didn't give him the right to do what he did. Even if it did feel like it was the right thing to do.

"Anya?" he called her name instantly getting her undivided attention. If he wasn't mistaken, it looked like she was holding her breath although her face was neutral. Just like him she was nervous about what was to come.

"I just want to apologize for what I did yesterday. I wasn't in my right frame of mind and I let my flesh take over. I was out of line and I hope you can forgive me."

"Bless you don't have to apologize. I understand that you weren't in a good head space with everything going on so you weren't thinking clearly," she told him before throwing the onions and peppers into the skillet. What she really wanted to tell him was that she had longed to be that close to him and share that connection since high school but she couldn't. It was inappropriate and not at all right in the eyes of God.

"I need to apologize to you though," she continued. "I'm sorry for not telling you who I was when I first came into the store. I knew instantly that it was you because there aren't many men named Bless, but I also saw your wedding ring. One thing about me is that I value the sanctity of marriage so I thought it was best that I not say anything. I didn't want any old feelings coming back up. If there were any feelings," she concluded.

"There were definitely feelings," was all that he said before the doorbell rang.

Assuming that it was Terrell or his parents Bless got up to open the door. The moment he did all of the rage that he was feeling previously had returned at the sight of Trinity standing in front of him with a look of disgust on her face.

"What are you doing here?" Bless almost yelled.

"I just came to get the signed divorce papers so that we can drop them off to the lawyer," she said nastily. The moment that she had said *'we'* Bless immediately focused his eyes on the brand new navy blue Maserati that sat in their driveway.

"You had to bring him to my house for this? That's so disrespectful," Bless said as he tried his best to control the anger that was about to erupt.

"No what's disrespectful is the fact that you talking about my man like it wasn't him who let you get that raggedy property to open your so called business. Oh and make sure that you pay on time to the bank. You wouldn't want them to foreclose on it," Trinity spat as if the words tasted like bile coming out.

"Bless doesn't have to worry about foreclosure because he didn't take out a loan he paid for it in cash," Anya stepped up behind him. She hadn't intended on making her presence known but she could hear the frustration and anger in Bless as he spoke and it was only a matter of time before he was about to go off. He didn't need that especially with Dre sitting in the car looking like he was waiting for something to jump off.

From where Anya was when the doorbell rang she could see out front and recognized the car that was parked instantly. She was going to warn Bless before he opened the door but he reached it before she could say anything. Now that she was privy to the situation and everyone involved, her discernment picked up on something that she should have noticed when she first met Emmanuel Andre Dennis. He had the same look in his eyes and the way that he carried himself just like her ex and she could bet her life on the fact that Trinity was in the same boat that she was once in.

The look on Trinity's face was priceless with the revelation that Bless actually had the money to pay for his new property. Or maybe it was because of Anya being there at the house that she once lived in so early in the morning. Because there was no other car in the driveway she didn't know he wasn't alone. When Dre suggested, or more like forced her to go and get the papers part of her was hesitant but then she thought it would serve Bless right to see her pull up in an expensive car with her new man. She was going to show him just how a real man was supposed to roll.

"Anya can you please go and get Ms. Marshall the papers off of my dresser. You know where the room is," Bless said being petty. Anya understood how he was feeling but she wasn't about to let him make reference to her in a way that suggested something that wasn't.

"Oh you jumped in his bed already? I guess fat homewreckers have to get it anyway that they can huh?" Trinity said rudely with her mouth turned up into a snarl.

Anya stopped abruptly and laughed before continuing to make her way up the stairs unbothered. Putting a little extra in her walk she went to do as she was asked and came back down the stairs. No matter how bad she wanted to slap that smug look off of Trinity's face she simply reached the divorce papers out to her. Snatching the papers Trinity flipped through them just to make sure that everything was signed and she was actually surprised that they were. She just knew that Bless was going to put up a fight about signing them and try to work things out so when he didn't start his begging and groveling like he usually did, to say that she was shocked was an understatement.

"You have what you came for now leave. There is no reason for you to be here any longer," Anya stated.

"Look at you trying to be the woman of the house and take my place."

"Sweetie let's be real this was always my place and you know it. That's why you went through all of the trouble that you did. But don't worry I got it from here. Whether I'm just Bless' friend or his woman you better believe that he won't ever have to worry about being hurt again," she said to a shocked Trinity. Movement from behind Trinity caused her to stop talking for just a moment before she started back. "But it looks like you better hurry up and leave before you need a little more concealer around the eyes don't you think?" Anya clapped back causing Trinity to absentmindedly raise her hand to her face before turning on her heals and rushing off. The last thing she needed and wanted was for Dre to get out of the car.

Hopping in on the passenger side Trinity put the divorce papers in Dre's lap and buckled her seatbelt. Pulling out of the driveway Dre accelerated the hundred thousand dollar car down the street. A part of her was furious that Dre didn't tell her that Bless paid cash for the property and the other part was trying to figure out where Bless had gotten the money from in the first place. He was always so frugal with money and she had access to the bank account that was negative too many times to count. That building that he had purchased was on the market for $165,000 but because it took so long to sell Dre let it go almost dirt cheap for 80 grand.

Whap! Whap!

Trinity was so deep into her thoughts that she didn't even have time to prepare herself for the two blows Dre had just delivered to her face. Anya may have just been being petty but she didn't know how true her statement was. The concealer to cover up the bruise around her eye must have been wearing off and starting to show.

"What did I do Dre?" Trinity cried.

"Didn't I tell you to just get the papers and leave. I said three minutes but you stood there running your big fat mouth for four minutes and twenty nine seconds," he stated calmly like him counting every second was normal.

Nothing he did was normal and Trinity was slowly starting to see that. But she couldn't be mad at him for hitting her. He had given clear instructions and because of Anya's big behind she had gotten side tracked. Now she had to walk on eggshells until Dre had calmed down and returned to the man that she fell in love with.

"I'm sorry baby but when I saw that big hog standing there I got mad."

"Yo, I don't know what you see but Anya is one beautiful woman. The way her body curves and sits up nicely I know Bless is gonna be banging that out soon," Dre laughed.

If it was one thing that Dre didn't care about it was what came out of his mouth. He didn't care if he hurt Trinity's feelings she would have to deal with it or else. Since she wanted to lie to him about being married he was going to make sure she felt his wrath. Dre wasn't like that towards her in the beginning. When he met Trinity he knew that she was the one that he wanted to be with. That was the whole reason behind him purchasing the home from Anya that he had but the moment he found out she was married when they were together he let his old demons out to play. Demons that no one knew that he had bottled up inside of him, especially Trinity. But she was sure finding out exactly who he was and it was too late to back out now. He may have only slapped her around and punched her in the face from time to time but nothing major. To him it wasn't even comparable to what he would do once his son was born and by then it would be way too late for Trinity to escape. She didn't realize how good she had it with Bless but there was nothing like a good eye opener, or in her case a closed and swollen eye, to remind her.

-16-

"Trinity where have you been?" her mother asked her over the phone. She had been trying to reach both Bless and her daughter for weeks now and neither were answering.

The last time Ernestine had spoken with either of them she knew that they were going through some serious issues but that was the last time they had talked. Her spirit was telling her that something was wrong but she couldn't get any answers. She had thought about reaching out to Bless' parents a few times but just in case they didn't know there was trouble in paradise she didn't want to let it be known. It was Bless and her daughter's jobs to share something like that.

"I've been busy mother," Trinity mumbled. It wasn't that she was trying to sound rude, which she knew her mother would take it that way anyway, but she had no choice because her mouth was swollen.

If Trinity had any idea how her lies would be affecting her right then she would have made sure to walk away from Bless a long time ago when she met Dre. He didn't deserve to be hurt by her so she understood exactly why he was taking his frustrations out on her. He didn't start right off hitting her after the incident at the café, a little shove here and a grab there. But now he was putting more force behind it and she deserved it.

"Busy with what? I know that you haven't been going to work like you are supposed to because I called your job so what are you busy with?" Ernestine let her know before she could even come up with the lie that she was working.

That old woman knew she was nosy.

"First of all," Trinity started only to be cut off by her mother.

"First of all," Ernestine repeated, "you better make sure you change your tone of voice and how you were about to speak to me before I reach through this phone and wrap your tongue around your neck. Now I done told you about the disrespect and I don't care how old you get. You will never be able to whip my behind!"

"Well if you stop trying to keep tabs on me like I'm still a child then I wouldn't have to check you about it. So if you must know I haven't been to work because this baby that I'm carrying is making me sick on the regular."

It was as if that last part of her sentence softened Ernestine and a smile as wide as the Nile formed across her face.

"Oh my God! How far along are you and why didn't you call and tell us when you found out? Jessie! Our baby is having a baby!" she laughed and got ready to break out into a shout. They had been waiting and praying that Trinity and Bless would have children for the longest and now their prayers were answered. Or so she thought.

"Do you really have to do all of that yelling in my ear? God I have a headache," Trinity whined. She wanted to be excited because her mother was but she knew that it was only a matter of time before good old Ernestine said something to ruin it.

"I'm sorry baby. I'm just so excited. I need to call Geneva so that we can start planning this baby shower! Have you and Bless told his parents yet?" Ernestine asked excitedly.

"No."

"No? Why not?"

"Why would I tell people that have nothing to do with this baby or me?" Trinity asked confusing her mother.

"Trinity what are you talking about? Why wouldn't they have anything to do with you or their grandchild?"

"Because it's not their grandchild!"

The only sound that could be heard was the one of her mother sucking in a sharp breath followed by silence. Tension between the phone lines felt so thick and Ernestine was at a loss for words. There was no way that her daughter was telling her that she was pregnant by another man while she was married to her husband.

"Yes mother I cheated on Bless with someone who is able to provide me with the life I deserve and because of that we are having a baby together. There is no repairing my marriage because the divorce is final and Dre and I will be getting married before our child gets here. Now I won't be as petty as you are so I will send you and daddy an invite. It's up to you if you decide to come or not and if you do please make sure that you respect my house and my man," Trinity let it be known.

"Well baby girl I hope you know what you have gotten yourself into. Don't worry about sending us an invite because I respectfully decline. There is no way that we will support something like this because of how you did it. Maybe this Dre character's parents will be enough for you. I pray God has mercy on your soul Trin," Ernestine said defeated before hanging up.

There was nothing else that needed to be said by either of them. She would always love her child but that didn't mean that she could condone her actions. Whoever this Dre person was Ernestine just hoped that he was worth the lifetime of hell that Trinity was about to endure and she prayed that her grandchild wouldn't suffer.

Placing the phone back on the nightstand beside her bed Trinity thought about something that her mother had said about Dre's parents. The two of them had been going on three years in a relationship, were about to get married, and had a baby on the way but she had never met his parents. There were plenty of times when she had asked to meet them and he told her in due time but it had yet to happen. Was he ashamed of her? Did he not see her as worthy enough to meet them? All of thoughts went through her head but still she trusted him and his decisions. She had to realize that just because Bless had been excited to introduce her to his parents that that didn't mean a thing. When she had finally met them it was clear that they weren't too fond of her so maybe Dre was justified with his reasoning. When it was the right time he would let her know and there was no doubt in her mind that they would love her just as much as he did.

"Who was that on the phone that's causing you to smile like that?" Dre asked. The look on his face was one that had become very familiar to Trinity.

"It was my mother. She called me because she hasn't heard from me in a while and I told her about the baby. Her and daddy are so excited and they can't wait to meet you," Trinity lied. There was no way that she was going to tell him the truth about how they really felt and when it came time to introduce them, she was sure that she could come up with some lie so they didn't have to.

In one swift motion Dre made his way from the doorway to the bed in record time before lifting her completely up off the bed by her neck. Trinity tried her best to release his fingers from her throat but he was too strong for her.

"Listen to me and listen to me good Trinity. Let this be the last time you lie to me. I heard the whole conversation between you and your mother. If she doesn't care for me then she doesn't care for you so she won't have to worry about seeing me, my child, or you. I hope her holier than thou behind enjoyed her last conversation with you because after today they are cut off from your life do you hear me?" he made clear through gritted teeth.

Trinity tried her best to nod her head in agreement but his grip was too strong and she was beginning to lose oxygen to her lungs. Just as she thought she was about to slip into unconsciousness he released her causing her to collapse on the bed. Her lungs felt as if she was inhaling balls of fire as she tried to get air into her body. All she could do was watch him as he watched her with no remorse and hope that she didn't do anything further to upset him. She knew that he was under a lot of pressure at work and the last thing that she wanted to do was add to his stress. From then on out she would have to make sure that she was the perfect fiancé and mother to his child because he deserved that and so much more.

-17-

Anya sat in front of her computer at work putting in the final numbers for a house that she was working on selling. It hadn't gone a smooth as she had liked for it to between the buyer and seller but with her skill she was able to get them both to agree on a number that pleased them both. Just as she completed what she needed to and sent the documents over by email there was a knock at her door.

"Come in," she called out to whoever it was.

"Hey boo," Cassie said coming into her office.

The tone of her voice didn't match the look on her face and Anya could see that something was bothering her. Since everything had gone on with Bless, Cassie had been out of the office and neither of them had bothered to contact the other. Anya was trying to get her thoughts and feelings together and Cassie was dealing with her own issues. Ones that she had caused.

"What's wrong Cass?" Anya asked concerned.

Plopping down in the chair across from Anya Cassie let out a deep breath and was about to speak when there was yet another knock at the door.

"It's open."

"Hey An these were just delivered for you," the receptionist Kimmie said with a huge smile spread across her pretty tanned face. Although Anya didn't mention it and wouldn't, she noticed as Cassie tried to roll her eyes discreetly.

Anya stood up to assist Kimmie with the red box that read *Venus ET Fleur* on the front as she sat the Edible Arrangement on the table beside her desk.

"Who sent these?" Anya asked before removing the top to the box and having her breath taken away at the sight before her.

Inside of the box were two dozen gold roses and a card that sat on top.

"Ooohhh girl I thought that's what this was! I saw these on Instagram and they are supposed to last at least a year. They cost a grip too so who is the secret admirer?" Kimmie asked excitedly.

"Probably one of those men that be buying all of those houses from her," Cassie sucked her teeth. Anya and Kimmie both looked at her to see what she was implying and immediately she tried to backpedal.

"I didn't mean it like that. I'm just saying that one of them were probably just thanking you for all that you have done for them," she tried to correct herself.

Neither Kimmie nor Anya was buying what she

had said because the statement was full of jealousy and Anya didn't know why. She had never had any real issues with Cassie so for her to be acting the way that she was threw her for a loop.

"Mmm hmm, anyway read the card," Kimmie said.

She had never been close with Cassie and it was for a good reason. Cassie was as low down and two faced as they came. Plenty of times as Kimmie sat at her desk she would hear Cassie talking with a few of the other agents about Anya but she had never wanted to be the one to go running back and starting trouble so she never said anything. They were mad that Anya was one of the best agents that worked there and she got her sales strictly because she was blessed at what she did and she didn't have to sleep her way to a sale like the others. Including Cassie. Married or not Cassie got her money any way that she knew how. But that was none of her business.

"I've never done this before so I pray that I'm doing this right. I remember your favorite colors were red and gold so I hope that you like the gifts. If so would you mind thanking me by going out to dinner with me?" Anya read the message on the card.

Her heart and stomach were full of butterflies and she couldn't stop the tears from forming. She had had plenty of suitors send her flowers or gifts but none of them meant as much as the ones that she had just received. It was as if everything was right in her world.

"Bless sent these?!" Cassie screeched while she snatched the card from between Anya's fingers.

Anya purposely didn't want to tell who had sent them while Cassie was in the room just because of the reaction that she had given. She wanted to avoid another hypocritical lesson on how it wasn't right to entertain a married man.

"Listen it's not what you are thinking Cass," Anya tried explaining only to get cut off.

"Oh it's exactly what I'm thinking. You are trying to get Bless in your bed! Wait until I tell my cousin," Cassie blurted out before realizing what she had said. Covering her mouth with her free hand her eyes bucked at her slip up.

Anya stared at Cassie for a few moments trying to understand what her 'friend' was talking about. Since Cassie hadn't spoken with Trinity in close to two months she had no idea about everything that had gone down between her and Bless. Even still she didn't want Anya to know that she was the same one who had helped Trinity end the relationship between the two of them.

"Your cousin?" Anya whispered more to herself than to anyone else. The day that Trinity had blurted out her secret she never did say who her cousin was. Because of the tension and emotions being on high, Anya didn't think to even ask who the cousin was and she surely didn't think that it was Cassie. Kimmie just stood there not knowing if she should leave the room or stay just in case she had to referee because she could now feel the heat of anger radiating from Anya's body before she spoke again.

"It's was you! All of this time I was thinking that you were telling me the things about Bless because you didn't want me breaking up a happy home. Not that I would ever be as low as you to do something like that. But you were doing it because you knew what you had done all of those years ago with Trinity. I can't believe this," Anya almost yelled. She tried so hard to keep her composure because the last thing she wanted to do was cause a scene at her place of employment. She wouldn't dare give the rest of the agents there the satisfaction of seeing her sweat. It was bad enough Cassie had to know her business.

"Girl please. What could Bless have done for you? My cousin and I saved you from being with a man that wasn't about nothing in the first place," Cassie sucked her teeth. Her whole demeanor had changed and the woman standing before Anya wasn't the one she was used to.

Sure Cassie had her ways and Anya knew that she

was sneaky to a certain extent but never in a million years would she have thought that this was how she really was. Her true colors were definitely out and as bright as day.

"So he wasn't good enough for me but he was good enough for Trinity? All of these years I missed out on the man I was supposed to be with because of your greedy, self-centered, bougie behind cousin?"

Kimmie stood there wanting so bad to ask questions to find out exactly what was going on because the tea that was being poured was super hot. Who was Bless and what was going on. The way that the two women before her were huffing and puffing across the room from one another she knew that if someone didn't leave it was going to come to blows.

"Wait until I tell my cousin that her husband and his fat fling from the past are creeping behind her back!"

"Sweetie is that the only insult that you and your cousin can try and throw at me? If I was insecure about my looks then maybe it would bother me but considering that neither of you can touch me on my worst day I'll let y'all feel like you said something. But let's be clear boo. Trinity and Bless are divorced and I'm getting the man that God intended for me to have before you and Satan's spawn decided that you wanted to play match maker. Now if you don't mind I need to call my future man and let him know what time to pick me up. See your way out or I'm sure Kimmie won't mind escorting you," Anya snapped.

Cassie stood there still stuck on the fact that Anya said Trinity and Bless were divorced. When did that happen and why wasn't she notified of it. Anya had to be lying and making stuff up to save face for getting caught creeping. That ad to be it and she was about to go and call Trinity and let her in on what her no good broke husband was doing behind her back.

"Did you hear her? Keep it moving heffa," Kimmie interrupted Cassie's thoughts.

"Oh so you trying to use that white privilege card thinking that you have some authority over me huh? Well sweetie let me tell you something. Maybe if you use that mouth a little more on old man Simpson instead of speaking like you are superior to me then maybe he will move you up to something other than just a receptionist," Cassie spat.

"And maybe if you just gather your things and leave now I won't have to tell my father, old man Simpson, and you won't have to be escorted out by security. I'm sure that would be embarrassing," Kimmie said shocking both Anya and Cassie. No one knew that Kimmie was the daughter of the CEO but they certainly did now. All of the color seemed to drain from Cassie's face at that moment.

"Your *father*?" Cassie said as her voice cracked.

If she lost this job then she would have to be solely dependent on her husband who wasn't in the same financial place that he was when she first met him. The man that she pursued while he was still with his wife was the same one that wined and dined her until his wife found out and divorced him. The moment that she had become First Lady things changed for them and she was glad that she had kept her job as an agent. Leron was paying out alimony as well as child support to his ex-wife so what little money he was able to keep he made sure to save it for a rainy day. Cassie wouldn't dare leave him and risk dealing with the 'I told you so's' from not just her family but the congregation that had decided to stick around after the scandal broke. They knew that it would only be a matter of time before God allowed that travesty of a marriage to end and they couldn't wait. Cassie would never give them the satisfaction. Her pride wouldn't let her. So instead of responding any further she turned on her heels and headed to her office to pack her things up.

-18-

Anya stood in her mirror and inspected the outfit that she had on. Normally she wouldn't stress about what she wore because she knew that she could pull off just about any look that she put together but tonight was different. It was her official date with Bless. The last time that she had seen him had been almost two months ago and it was for good reason. After the night they spent together and the kiss they had shared she felt that it was best to stay away because her feelings were clouding her judgement. The last thing that she wanted to happen was Bless take her as just a rebound because he was still hurt but trying his best to move on. That's not how she wanted things between them so she stayed away. She still went by to spend time with Ronda and the baby but as soon as she found out that Bless would be stopping by she would leave before he got there.

When she called to let him know that she would love to go out with him the smile in his voice let her know that he was feeling the same type of excitement that she was feeling. So her outfit of choice had to be flawless even if she didn't know where they were going. He told her to be comfortable and ready to have fun but that could mean anything. She looked at her white long sleeved crop top that showed just a little bit of her stomach, the light denim jeans hugged her curves, and her gold sandals went well with the gold jewelry she wore. Today her hair was braided in a thick halo braid with a few curly strands sticking out and her baby hair was popping! Anya decided not to wear any heavy makeup but she did coat her lips with some lip gloss and after spraying her body with her Dolce and Gabbana perfume she headed to her living room to wait.

It was too early for dinner so Anya wondered why he told her to be ready by 2pm. Every minute she was looking down at either her watch or phone to check the time and the closer it got to time the more her nerves kicked in. Just at the second hand hit the 12, her doorbell rang and it felt like her heart dropped to the bottom of her stomach.

"Get it together boo. This isn't your first time being around Bless. Just be you 'cause you got this!" she gave herself a small pep talk right before she opened the door.

This man just seemed to get finer every time she saw him and that should have been a sin. The way he had his dreads falling down his back and around his broad muscular shoulders made her want to run her fingers through his head. Her eyes roamed down his body and took in his appearance. It was funny that they were dressed alike with him in a white polo shirt, jean shorts, and tan Sperry's on his feet.

"I see you tried to match my fly huh?" Bless said causing them to share a laugh with his deep dimples on display.

Lord those dimples!

"Not that it was planned but I don't think that's such a bad thing."

To Bless confidence radiated off of Anya but in her mind she was about to lose her mind. This was the first time that they would be alone together for personal reasons and she was excited yet a little scared about what that would mean.

"You ready beautiful?"

"Yeah let me get my purse and keys," she told him as she blushed. Just him calling her beautiful had her screaming on the inside.

Once she was done locking up he walked her over to his truck and opened the passenger door for her before making his way to the other side of the truck. If Anya knew the feelings that he was feeling on the inside she would probably think he was crazy but he couldn't believe that he finally had the woman that he wanted by his side. Granted this was their first official date with one another but he knew that if he played his cards right and God was on his side there would be many more to come.

When she opened the door looking as beautiful as ever his heart skipped a few beats and he was almost tongue tied. But being the OG triple OG that he was he pulled it together.

"So where are we going?" Anya inquired as she stared at him with those gorgeous brown eyes of hers.

"I have a few surprises up my sleeve today. You trust me?" he asked.

"With my life," was her honest answer. Wait. Did she say that out loud?

"Well I'll go to the ends of the earth to make sure that life is protected."

What in the world was going on? Things were moving way too fast for them to be disclosing their feelings like that or was it. It wasn't like they had never said things to each other back in the day but that was just puppy love right? Whatever it was Anya and Bless were both there for it. If this was in God's plan for them, this day was the beginning of the best days of their lives.

***

"Oh my God Bless! Are you serious right now?" Anya screamed before snatching her seatbelt off and jumping out of the car before it could come to a complete stop.

"Yo An be careful ma," he said concerned getting out right behind her.

Bless walked up behind her and just stood there admiring her as she covered her mouth and tears formed in her eyes.

"I can't believe you did it so fast," she told him in awe as she looked at the brand new store. Everything was already in place with only a few minor things that needed to be done but that would take no time to complete.

"I been working day and night to get it together and by the grace of God and help from my pops, Terrell, and some of the men from church we were able to move pretty fast. I plan on doing a ribbon ceremony in two weeks and I want you by my side," he told her as he took her hand.

She was shaking like a leaf and he didn't know if it

was a good or bad thing. But one thing he did know for sure was that he didn't want anyone else by his side than the one woman that had believed in him from the beginning. Because of her and the help that she provided he was able to do the one thing that he had always wanted and that was to become a business owner. No more working for anyone else but himself and the family that he had hoped to one day have.

"Really?" she asked him shocked but excited at the same time. It would be her honor to accompany him to something so important to him and by the look in his eyes he wasn't going to take no for an answer.

"Of course. Who would be better than the woman that believed in me?"

After taking about twenty minutes to give her a tour they were on their way to the next destination. They talked about everything under the sun it seemed like and the chemistry was definitely there. When they pulled up to the indoor go karting track Anya got a little uncomfortable and Bless could sense her hesitation.

"What's wrong?" He asked her concerned.

"Nothing," she lied as she reached for the door handle at the same time that he reached over to stop her.

"One thing about me An is that I'm a communicator. If there is something wrong I want to know what it is before it gets out of hand. I know things may be happening kind of fast but if we are going to build anything, friendship or something more, then we can't be afraid to talk to one another. I've been through that once before and I don't want to go backwards."

Seeing the sincerity in his eyes, Anya let out a deep breath and spoke.

"My fiancé was the type that was physically, mentally, emotionally, and verbally abusive to me. I stayed because at the time my self-esteem wasn't as high as it is now so I let him get away with things that I shouldn't have. He held so much over my head back then. Anyway, he took me out one day to a place like this because I had always wanted to do go kart racing. Once we got inside I felt like everyone was looking at me because granted I was a little heavier back then. But I thought that it wouldn't be an issue. So when we went to get our tickets the girl behind the counter looked at me with a smirk on her face and told me flat out that I was too big. Instead of him standing there and taking up for me, he joined in on the giggles and told her to just give him a ticket and my big behind could watch. I would probably slow the kart down anyway," she explained not realizing that she had begun to cry. Had she put on makeup earlier her face would be ruined.

Bless took his hand and cupped her face as he wiped the tears away with his thumb and looked at her.

"Listen to me and listen to me good. There is nothing wrong with the size you are or were. You are beautiful inside and out and as long as you are healthy that's all that matters to me. The confidence that you have and how you carry yourself is one of the sexiest things that I have ever seen. I don't mean to sound like I'm comparing you to Trinity but all she ever did was pile weave on top of weave on her head and cake on so much makeup that half of the time I forgot what she looked like. But you, you are naturally beautiful and you know that you don't need all of that to make yourself appealing. Buddy just couldn't appreciate the goddess that God created you to be because you weren't created for him. God created you from my rib and as long as you will let me you will never have to ever feel like you are less than again. I dare anyone to come out of their mouth negatively about you. You can bet money that it won't be pretty. Do you hear me?" he let it be known.

If Anya wasn't in love before she definitely was now. The words that Bless spoke to her were filled with so much passion and honesty that it took her breath away. She couldn't even for the word 'yes' to respond so all she did was smile and nod her head.

"Come here," he instructed softly as he pulled her close to him before planting a kiss on her forehead. Then her nose. Then her cheeks. And finally, her lips. Everything that man did was new to her and he was definitely one of a kind. Anya knew in that moment that if he was committed to her then she was certainly going to be committed to him.

The kiss lasted so long and made her feel weak and energized all at the same time. He just had that effect on her. He just admired her for a while before they got out and headed inside. For the next two hours they rode around and laughed like big kids having the time of their lives before finally going to dinner. Bless pulled out all of the stops for her and made a promise that if she just held on there would be so many days like that to come.

-19-

Six Months Later…

Bless stood beside Anya with Terrell and Ronda as they dedicated their baby back to the Lord. As promised they were given one of the most important roles in a child's life after the parents and they welcomed being baby Anya's Godparents. It was their job to make sure that she knew who the Lord was and were taught His ways and in the untimely even that something happened to her parents they would raise her as their own. Most people acted like a God parent was just someone who would babysit and spoil their child when it was deeper and more scared than that.

Once the ceremony was over and all of the other babies were dedicated as well Matthew gave a powerful word. And maybe Bless would have known what the topic was about if he had been paying attention but he wasn't. His mind had wandered off thinking about the woman that sat beside him and he could help it.

Reaching over he took her hand in his and smiled at her. For the last six months they had been getting closer than he could have ever imagined and he knew what the next step for them would be. He had just hoped that she was on the same page as he was. Day in and day out Bless spent time talking to and thanking God for all that He had done in his life. His business was doing great, his spiritual life was better than it had ever been, and his relationship with Anya was flourishing. Bless was indeed blessed.

He was so deep in thought that he hadn't even realized that his father was giving the benediction and letting everyone go to spend the rest of their day with family and friends.

"Babe come on," she said tugging on his arm to get him to stand. They walked around and said fellowshipped a few minutes before his parents walked over to them.

"There go my baby," his mother said extending her arms to what he thought was him. Instead they wrapped around Anya and he couldn't help but laugh.

"Dang ma I thought I was your baby," he faked like he was hurt.

"Oh hush you know you my big baby but Anya is my boo," she smiled.

The relationship that his parents had with Anya was nothing like the one they had with Trinity or the lack thereof. She had joined the church and was one of the youth pastors in their children's church where the kids adored her. Every member spoke so highly of her and what stuck out to them the most was how genuine she was. Nothing she did was for show because she had the heart of God.

"We still doing dinner later?" his father inquired. He was hoping that it would be later on in the day because right then he needed his nap.

"As soon as Anya comes back from making a visit to Trinity's house," Bless informed them with no emotion whatsoever.

"Why do you have to go over to that wombat's house?" Geneva asked while scrunching up her nose.

"In the Lord's house Neva? Can we at least get outside before you start being petty?" Matthew asked.

"Sorry Jesus but you know she's a wombat," Geneva somewhat repented if that was what you could call it.

"Every six months we like to go by our client's house just to make sure that they are doing well in their new place and if they have any questions or concerns. Like a follow up. Something my boss has been doing since he started. I guess that's why our company gets as many referrals as we do because of that. Makes them feel special," Anya explained.

"That makes sense. So do you think that's something that you can handle considering the circumstances?" Matthew asked.

"Yeah. I don't have any issues and this is part of my job. As long as they allow me to continue to be professional I will."

"Well can you teach this one here how to remain professional instead of being ready to set it off all of the time?" He joked.

"So what you trying to say Matthew? I know how to act," Geneva pouted like she was mad. She knew exactly what he was referring to and he was absolutely right. But that didn't mean that he had to call her out on it.

"Of course you do baby. We will see you all later on for dinner. I'm old so I need a nap," Bless' father said as he grabbed his mother's hand.

"Alright old man we'll be there. While Anya does her job I'm gonna stop by the store and check on things before heading over," he informed them all. It was an understatement how proud of him they were and they could tell by the way his eyes seemed to sparkle how happy he was. This dream of his may have felt like it was long overdue but Bless knew that it was right on time.

God's time.

They said their goodbyes before all heading out to go their separate ways. All the way to the house that Trinity and Dre now called their own Anya couldn't help but to pray for a good outcome. Unlike Bless she had been paying attention to the service and it was all about forgiveness. She knew in order to get past everything and move forward she had to forgive Trinity for what she had done years ago. Although it was a messed up thing for her to do out of selfishness, they were just kids. Who knew what would have transpired between her and Bless had they gotten together then. Maybe Trinity did them a favor and now was the right time.

Anya knew that some people may look at her crazy for how their new relationship began but her heart was pure and right with God. When she came back into Bless' life for the second time not one time did she set out to destroy his marriage and make him her own. Even when he found out what Trinity was doing behind his back she stayed away. Now that things had blown over and they had time to pray and think about their situation they agreed that with each other was where they wanted to be.

Anya had zoned so far out that she hadn't even realized that she made it to the house. It was a miracle that she had gotten there unscathed because she wasn't paying a lick of attention to the road. Taking a deep breath she noticed that only one car had been in the driveway. Thinking back to when she met Trinity that morning at the store she recognized it as the same BMW that she drove. Dre's car was MIA and she almost turned around. She didn't think that he would be an issue but she knew that Trinity wouldn't pass up the opportunity to be petty, still something on the inside of her made her get out.

Instead of taking everything out of the car Anya only grabbed her phone and keys before she locked her door. To the naked eye nothing looked to be out of place. The landscape was immaculately done just like every other house in the neighborhood and she could tell that now it had a woman's touch put on it. No matter how nice her surroundings looked, the feeling that lingered in the air was thick. She didn't know what it was but she just prayed that she made it out without any unnecessary issues. Just before she pressed the doorbell to alert anyone in the house of her presence she noticed that the front door was partially open. Had it been a snake to some it would have bit them because it wasn't very noticeable. But just like she always did she paid attention to details.

The smart thing would have been to hightail it back to her car and call the police but her feet were planted like they were weighed down in buckets of cement at the sight before her. Off to the left of the porch the venetian blinds were slightly opened and a partial right leg lay right by the entrance to the dining room. Whoever was on the floor wasn't visible from the top of their thigh up and against her better judgement she finally gathered herself and pushed the door open running full speed ahead.

"Oh God!" Anya gasped as she rounded the corner to find a very pregnant and badly bruised Trinity laying on the floor. The scene looked like something straight out of a horror movie and instantly flashbacks of her being in Trinity's position over took her brain.

Trinity was laid out with her right leg positioned normally but her left leg was bent at an awkward angle. Without a doubt Anya could tell that it was broken in more than one place. Trinity may not have been a good wife but she was beautiful on the outside. It was her insides that made her so ugly but with that being the case her face now matched her heart.

She was so light skinned but now almost all of her exposed body was a bluish-purple color and the blood…there was so much blood it could have been a slaughter house. The most blood though was pooling from under her lower half of her body and that alone made Anya spring into action.

Placing a call to 911 she put the phone on speaker as she ran over to check Trinity's pulse. The moment she lifted her left had she noticed a brand new princess cut wedding ring on her finger. Anya was in shock to know that she was married and wondered if Bless knew or if he even cared. That was the least of her concerns though because there was no doubt in her mind that he would ever get back with Trinity in this lifetime or the next.

"911 what's your emergency," the operator asked coming onto the line.

"Yes we need an ambulance. There is a pregnant woman badly beaten in her home. She has a pulse but I'm not sure if the baby is still alive because there is so much blood," Anya told her trying not to panic.

The operator asked for the address and let her know to stay on the phone until helped arrived and she agreed. She didn't know if it was a home invasion and if the culprits were still inside or if her suspicions about Dre were being confirmed. Either way she wasn't about to leave Trinity's side until someone got there. As crazy as it sounded, if Trinity or the baby would indeed pass from their injuries she didn't want them to be alone when it happened.

Since they were in an upscale neighborhood it wasn't a shock that sirens could be heard getting closer so fast. It was a good thing too because from the barely audible moans trying to escape Trinity's mouth if she didn't get to the hospital soon she may not make it.

"Just hold on Trinity. Help is here," Anya soothed

not completely sure if Trinity could even hear her or not.

"Hello?" an EMT called out.

"In here!" Anya yelled back to them.

The moment the two men saw her sprawled out on the floor they jumped into action while Anya moved out of the way. A few seconds later she heard heavy footsteps followed by the crackling sounds of a two way radio before the boys in blue walked in.

"Can you tell me what happened here?" the white officer asked. Normally Anya didn't judge a book by it's cover but he fit the description of the kind of police that had a chip on their shoulder. One that would shoot first and scream self-defense after he was done.

"I was making a house call to one of my clients and when I got here I saw the front door opened a little and then noticed a leg when I looked through the window," she told him as she pointed to the window that she had looked in earlier.

"Client?" he asked skeptical.

"Yes. I'm a real estate agent and I sold this house to her fiancé a while back. My boss requires us to follow up with them six months after just to make sure everything is going well," she explained. By the look on his face he wasn't buying it even though it was the truth but she didn't care one way or the other. She had no reason to lie and as soon as they told her she was free to go she would do just that.

"Hmm," was his simple reply but it was laced with something that Anya couldn't make out.

"How is she?" the other officer asked just as the medics strapped her to the stretcher and prepared to head out to the ambulance.

"Barely holding on and I'm not sure if the baby is still alive or not. I can't get a heartbeat on the Doppler. Excuse us but we need to go."

"Oh God no not another one," Anya said thinking about how her unborn child lost its life.

"What you just say?" Mr. Chip on his shoulder asked.

"Nothing. If that's all I need to go."

"We'll be in touch Ms…."

"O'Day. Anya O'Day."

"Well we will be in touch if we need any more information from you," he said staring at her with an ice cold glare that made her shiver all the way down to her bones.

Closing the door behind them everyone left out of the house and Anya got into her car. The first thing she did was pull out her phone to call someone but who? If

Dre had been the one to beat Trinity within inches of her life he most definitely wasn't the one that she needed to call but what if he wasn't responsible? From the looks of it she was now his wife and he deserved to know about the wellbeing of her and their unborn child. Still something wasn't right so she called the next best person that she could. Ronda.

"Hey sis you on the way to mommy's house?" Ronda inquired as soon as she answered the phone.

"Um not yet."

"Well girl you better hurry because these ribs, mac and cheese, fried cabbage, cornbread, and dark chocolate cake is smelling off. We can't eat until you get here."

"Is Bless there yet?" Anya asked ignoring the menu that was just called out to her. Any other time she would have been licking her lips and speeding down the road to get to Geneva's cooking but right then she didn't have even a small appetite.

"He just got here. What's wrong?" Ronda asked picking up on the tone of her voice.

"You know I had to come and do a follow up at Trinity's house," she started before Ronda cut her off.

"Don't tell me that troll tried you! Ohhhh she better be glad she's pregnant but when I see her it's going down. On sight I'm tagging that head," Ronda ranted.

"No no. She didn't try anything. When I got here the door was open and when I went to look into the window I saw a leg on the floor. I rushed in and it was her. She was beaten so bad sis. The EMTs said she was barely holding on and they couldn't get a heartbeat on the baby. They are rushing her to the hospital now and I think I'm going to go just to make sure she is alright," Anya said just as a knock on her window startled her.

Officer Chip.

Rolling her window down she put Ronda on hold to see what he was still doing there.

"Is there a reason why you haven't left the residence yet?" he asked with accusing eyes.

"Because I'm trying to get in touch with someone related to Trinity so they know what's going on."

Without another word he simply backed away and headed back to his car. Anya watched him for a few minutes in her rearview mirror as he talked to his partner with the two of them keeping their eyes on her as well. One thing she didn't have time for, was being a hashtag and ending up like Sandra Bland and so many other innocent victims of police killings. She buckled her seatbelt and pulled out of the driveway slowly in the direction of the hospital. Trinity may not have been one of her favorite people by a long shot but there was no way that she wouldn't send up a prayer on both her and her baby's behalf.

-20-

While Anya was talking to the officer and had placed her call on hold, Ronda was filling in everyone on what she had been told so far. Everyone in the house were shocked and though no one cared for Trinity at all that still didn't stop them from praying that she would be alright. No matter how evil of a person they thought she was she still didn't deserve that kind of treatment.

Once the news was out they all waited to see what Bless' reaction would be and if he would decide to go and check on her or not. No matter what she had been his wife for ten years up until six months ago and he had indeed loved her. They would understand if he wanted to make sure she was fine because they knew that there was no chance that he would get back with her but he wasn't heartless. That's what made him and Anya a strong couple.

For Anya to be as concerned as she was about Trinity after all that had transpired showed just the type of woman she was. Ronda could admit as she stood there waiting to see what would be said and done next, Anya was a better woman than she was. She wouldn't have cared one bit about going to sit at a hospital with Terrell's ex-wife if he had one and she was in the same situation. She would have called the ambulance and left it at that.

"Where's Anya?" Bless wanted to know.

"On her way to the hospital," Ronda told him.

"Let's go," he said suddenly before grabbing his keys and phone from the coffee table almost knocking his father over. It may have looked like he was rushing to Trinity's side but once he found out that his woman was headed up there he needed to be with her. He couldn't imagine how she must have been feeling about everything.

It took them a little over twenty minutes to reach the hospital and when they entered into the emergency room Bless spotted Anya first. She was sitting off in a corner to herself with her head slightly down and he could see the tears falling from her face as her mouth steadily moved. He knew that she was praying for Trinity and her baby and it did something to him. In that moment he felt like she was too good to be true because no matter how much she didn't care too much for Trinity because of everything that she had done, she could still find it in her heart to pray for her. That was a true sign of a person after God's own heart.

If everyone could put aside their personal differences and stand in the gap with prayer for the other when it was needed Bless felt like this would be a better world. But way too often people let their pride get in the way not caring if it was the right thing to do or not. It was right then that he knew that the decision he had made a while back was the right one. God had just given him the confirmation that he needed to move forward.

"An," Bless called out to her when he had gotten a few feet away from her.

Snapping her eyes open she quickly got out of her seat and ran right into his arms and broke down crying.

"Baby she looked so bad and they couldn't find the baby's heartbeat! Who would do something like that to her?" she cried into his chest.

"Shhhh bae it's going to be alright. Her and the baby will be just fine. It was a good thing you went by there when you did. Let's just keep praying and asking God for a miracle," Bless said lovingly as he caressed her back.

Bless understood just why the situation was taking its toll on Anya the way that it was. She had never told him everything that had happened to her when she lost her baby by the hands of her ex but Ronda had shared that with them on the way over. It crushed him to know that she had gone through something as heinous as being beat to the point where she almost died and her baby lost its life in the process. He never understood how a man could put his hands on a woman unless it was to express nothing but love to every inch of her body. No matter how upset he had ever gotten with Trinity or his father with his mother neither of them had ever laid a hand on their women and never would. Women were God's gift to the world and He expressed that when he presented her to Adam. She was given as a gift to him just Anya was given to him.

After about thirty more minutes of them waiting and praying the door that led to the back opened up at the same time Dre and Cassie came through the front entrance. Neither of them had seen one another since Cassie was fired but knowing that she and Trinity were related, she was the only choice that Anya had when she couldn't reach Dre. Bless wasn't sure if it was a good idea for them to remain there considering all that had gone down between them anyone but before he could speak on it someone else spoke first.

"Family of Trinity Dennis?" the little Asian doctor called out. She didn't look like she was a day over twenty five and fresh out of medical school.

From the confused looks on everyone's faces except Anya, it hit her that she didn't have time to even tell them she had gotten married. Not that it mattered because from the way Bless was carrying himself he didn't care one way or the other if she had moved on and that gave Anya even more confidence than she had before.

"Right here! I'm her husband and this is her cousin Cassandra," Dre said walking over to where she stood.

No one else joined them because they weren't family but they were close enough to hear what was being said. Once they found out her condition then they would all go about their day.

"I'm Dr. Kobiyoshi and I'm the physician that was here when your wife was brought in. She was beat up pretty badly and because of that we had to rush her upstairs to the operating room. Her injuries were extensive which caused us to have to deliver your daughter by cesarean. She is full term but because her mother was so badly beaten she was affected as well and is in the NICU. Your wife had to be placed in a medically induced coma in order for her body to try and recover. It's touch and go right now but we are going to do everything that we can for them," she explained before asking if they had any questions.

Hearing that Trinity and her baby girl might not make it caused everyone in the room to feel some type of sadness. Neither her or the baby deserved that. Knowing that there was no need for them to stay there, everyone began making their way to the door before Anya was stopped once again by the same officer.

"Ms. O'day why are you here?" he asked her.

Bless didn't like the tone of his voice and to him

he sounded just a little too accusatory for his liking.

"Is it against the law to come and check to make sure that Trinity and her baby are alright considering I was the one that found them?" she asked.

"Found them or assaulted them?" they heard Cassie speak from behind them.

"Excuse me? Who are you and what do you mean by assaulted them?" the other officer finally spoke up.

"I'm Trinity's cousin and what I mean is she probably had something to do with my cousin laying up in here fighting for her life. Oh I bet you didn't know that Anya is the reason that her first marriage ended. She just couldn't let well enough alone," Cassie lied right through her teeth.

"I know this ole broke down street walking so called First Lady didn't!" Ronda yelled but before she could go any further Bless stepped in.

"Officer that's a lie. I'm Trinity's ex-husband and Anya had nothing to do with my marriage ending or what happened today," he confirmed.

"Well it's pretty convenient how she was the one that found them, she was the one that came into their lives wreaking havoc, and she is the one with blood on her clothes," Dre revealed causing everyone to immediately look down at the blood that was located on the bottom of her dress. It wasn't a lot to cause someone to notice right away but now that it was pointed out it made her look like she was covered in blood. Still no one believed that she was responsible, well there was one.

"Come on now Cassidy. You know me and you know that I wouldn't do something like that. If I did why would I call you to let you know?" Anya asked as calmly as possible. There was nothing that made her blood boil faster than someone lying on her. She didn't do it to others and didn't want anyone doing it to her.

"All I know is that my cousin and her baby are fighting for their lives and you are the bitter side chick. Makes perfect sense to me," Cassie shrugged her shoulders.

Before Anya could even respond she felt her arms being placed behind her back before the cold sensation of metal wrapped around her wrists.

"Ms. O'day you have the right to remain silent," the narcissist of an officer began reading her rights.

"What? I didn't do anything. I was the one that helped her for Christ's sake," Anya tried explaining along with Bless, his parents, Terrell, and Ronda.

"Anything you say can and will be used against you in the court of law."

"Baby don't worry I'll be right there to get you,"

Bless called out behind her. He couldn't believe that this was happening to Anya and for what? There was no way that she did what they were accusing her of and how could they take the word of someone off the streets. Family or not Cassie was just as trifling as her cousin and it would only be a matter of time before she was reaping what she had sown as well.

While the first officer led Anya to the car with everyone else trailing behind them trying to vouch for her, the second officer remained inside to speak with the doctor. He didn't agree one bit with how his partner was carrying on but that's just how Grady rolled and he couldn't stand it. They had nothing to go on to point fingers towards Anya but the words of a family member who didn't witness the beating. A family member he already didn't trust.

-21-

The smell of year old urine, vomit, and sweat filled the tiny space that held Anya and twenty other women. She was cold and hungry and just wanted to be home in her bed but here she was not knowing how long she would be sitting inside of the holding cell. Bless promised that he would be there to get her out but she had no clue if he was going to be able to or not. The guards wouldn't let her get her one phone call to even see so she was stuck praying and wondering.

"Would you shut up all that mumbling? Ain't no God so I don't know why you wasting your time praying. If He was real wouldn't none of us be in here," she spat.

"Shut up Bertha!" another woman yelled at her and that caused them to begin a shouting match. Anya didn't care what they were arguing about as long as they didn't get to swinging and made a mistake and hit her. The space wasn't big enough for all of that and she was over the whole ordeal. She needed someone to come and get her out before she had to revert back to her fighting days. The way some of those women were looking at her she knew that it would only be a matter of time before she had to show them that she was saved but they could still catch those hands.

"O'day!" she heard her name called and jumped up like her butt was on fire.

"Right here," she said way to eagerly.

"I don't know what you so excited for. The only reason they calling your name is because they found you a jumpsuit big enough to fit your big behind," Bertha laughed.

Before Anya could turn around and clap back on Bertha the lady from earlier popped off again.

"You just mad that on her worst day you can't touch her. Over there looking like Master Yoda's grandma. Ugly self!"

That was it. Just as the guard unlocked the door Bertha hauled off and hit the other woman and she took it like it was a love tap. But the one she returned almost knocked Bertha through the wall. Indeed Bertha was a burly woman and towered over the other but she was quick and strong making up for what she lacked in weight and height. Anya almost stood there to watch and see who was going to win until the male guard pulled her by her arm to the outside of the cell while three other guards went in to break up the fight.

"The charges have been dropped against you. All I need is for you to sign these release papers and you are free to go," Officer Walker told her.

He was a handsome older man, like he was around her daddy's age, but she could tell that he went to the gym faithfully. Or maybe just being in there having to deal with the inmates kept him in shape. Whatever it was he looked healthy.

"That's it?" she asked him.

"Yep that's it. You are free to go. They will contact you for a court date by mail only if the charges aren't dropped. Between you and I the charges have a pretty good chance of being dropped."

"How do you know?"

"Well there really isn't any evidence tying you to what happened and the officer that arrested you didn't follow protocol. Now if the victim says otherwise then that's when they will move forward. But I serve a mighty God and from what I can tell so do you. So get on up out of here. Your boyfriend is waiting on you out front. He's a lucky man," the officer told her and winked his eye at her. It wasn't in that creepy old man wanting a young girl kind of wink but more as if he was giving her confirmation about Bless in some way. At least that was how she chose to take it. Just knowing that Bless kept his promise and came to her aid made her heart swell even more with love for him.

"Thank you so much and you have a blessed day," she told him before following the directions to the front of the jail.

The moment her eyes landed on Bless she couldn't contain the tears that began to flow. Sensing her presence Bless looked over into her direction and as soon as he saw her crying he rushed to her.

"Anya you ok baby? Did they hurt you in here?" he asked with both his eyes and voice filled with concern.

"No, no I'm fine. Just glad to see you," she let him know. He looked like if she had said anything other than she was fine he was going to set it off causing her to smile through her happy tears.

"You sure?" he wanted to know for clarity.

"Yes babe I'm fine. Can we please go so I can shower and just relax? This was too much."

Looking at her once again to make sure that she was being honest with him he then took her hand and led her out of the front doors. Now that she was back in his life he was going to protect her at all costs just like he had done for Trinity. But things were different now because he knew that unlike Trinity, Anya would be appreciative of his efforts as the man in her life.

"I can't believe Cassie did that to me," Anya told him once he got in on his side.

"I can. She's always been that type. I just can't believe how small this world really is," he said as he looked behind him before pulling out.

It still amazed him that after all the time that he had been hearing about Cass from Anya, she was in fact the same Cass that he had gone to school with and was related to by marriage. They rarely saw each other because honestly Bless didn't care for her so there was no way to even know she was the same person.

The two of them rode in silence on the way to her house. Since she had gotten arrested Bless decided to cancel their dinner date with his parents and take her home. He knew that she would probably want to shower and change after being in that cell even if it was only for a few hours. A second was too long as far as he was concerned and it still bugged him that it had happened.

"I'm sorry that you had to go through this," Bless apologized even though she felt that he had no reason to. It wasn't his fault that any of this had happened to her so he didn't need to take responsibility for it.

"You have nothing to do with this," Anya replied while taking his right hand in her left and intertwining their fingers. "This was all Cassie. I should have known something was up all the times that she would have so much to say about you when she has her own skeletons to deal with."

"You told her about me?" he asked glancing quickly at her face before returning his eyes to the road. This was the first time that he had heard of Anya saying anything about him to anyone else.

"Against my better judgement I told her about the one man that I was in love with but couldn't have. I ran down the entire story about how we met and how we ended. She was the only friend that I had, or so I thought, so I felt like if I didn't tell someone about what was going on with me then I would break down.

At first, she didn't know who I was talking about because I never said your name and she was all for me getting my man back. But as time went along and the more I told her she slowly changed her instructions. I should have picked up on it way before now."

"If we both had picked up on her and her trifling cousin then we wouldn't be in this situation," Bless told her. He kicked himself daily after finding out about Trinity and her secret life because he should have been smarter than what he was back then. He knew he should have listened to that still small voice in his head but his eyes blinded him. Trinity had a way to make him forget about everything and everyone but that was only so that she could pull the wool over his head. Trinity may have fooled him but there was no way that God was fooled one bit and she was starting to reap just what she had sown.

-22-

"Good morning beautiful," Cassie heard while her head was still under the covers. All she needed was a few more hours a rest and she would be ready to start her day.

Throwing the covers back she looked up and smiled. Her husband Leron was one fine man and in the bedroom he was nothing like he was out in the streets. But the way Dre stood before her in nothing but the skin he was born in did something to her.

"Hey handsome," she smiled as he leaned in for a kiss.

Cassie's body shivered involuntarily under his touch like he had her under a spell. When she thought about it she kind of was. No matter how much she tried not to be she couldn't help it and wasn't about to apologize for it. Unlike Anya, it didn't matter to Cassie about taking someone else's man because that was just what she did. Both she and Trinity felt that if a man could be taken from his woman then he wasn't theirs to begin with. Nothing pleased her more than the chase and knowing that she could have her cake and eat it too. Besides, isn't that what cake was for? To eat.

The moment that Cassie met Dre she knew that she had to have him. Cousin or not the look he gave her confirmed that she wasn't the only one thinking the same thing. It took them a while to make things happen between them because Trinity picked up on everything but the further along she got in her pregnancy the less she could do. Every time Dre could see her she would lie to her husband and tell him that she was going to do 'ministry'. If he only knew that this bedroom ministry that she was doing had nothing to do with God. Even though she called out to Him on the regular in the heat of passion.

Trinity was the one to blame for how Cassie ended up sleeping with Dre and having him lace her pockets but she conveniently left out the part about him using her as a punching bag. If she hadn't been talking about how good he was in bed or how much money he had at her disposal she wouldn't have paid him any mind. Now her head was too far gone for Dre and she had her cousin to thank for that. The two of them may have been close but Cassie was closer to that almighty dollar. For the love of money was the root of all evil and Cassie couldn't agree more. That was one scripture that was relevant to her. Everything else in that boring book was a bunch of fluff and shenanigans let her tell it. So many times Anya would talk about how people would break apart the word just to fit their situation or circumstance. But oh well to each his own.

Thinking of Anya caused a sinister smile to cross

her face as she thought about how she had lied to the police. She had to do something to get back at her for costing her her job. Of course she knew that Anya wouldn't hurt a fly but her petty meter was at a staggering high.

"What are you smiling at?" Dre's deep baritone voice caressed her ears.

"Just thinking about how Anya's big behind is sitting behind bars because of me."

"What is it with you skinny broads always calling a sexy plus sized woman fat? Does her perfection intimidate you?" Dre asked getting off the bed disgusted.

To him when a woman always had something negative to say about the next she was insecure. Especially when the one they call themselves degrading was on such a higher level than they were. Anya was one of the most beautiful women that he had ever laid eyes on in his life and he understood why any man would want to have her all to himself. But he wouldn't be one of them. The women that he decided to get involved with were weak so that meant that he could treat them exactly how he wanted to. He could tell the day that he met Anya that she was strong and wouldn't stand for how he treated her so he passed.

"I know you didn't! Baby trust there is nothing that intimidates me especially not her," she lied.

Anya was everything she wasn't and that was clear to both Cassie and Trinity. Just from the confidence alone that Anya possessed spoke volumes. She wasn't impressed with how much money a man had because she had her own, she didn't let people run all over her, and she may have been bigger than what society preferred that made no difference to her. She could shut down any runway with her beauty and sense of style. But most of all it was clear that she had the favor of God over her life.

"So if she doesn't intimidate you why the name calling?"

"I'm just calling a cow a cow."

"Whatever. But I do appreciate you taking the heat off of me," Dre said as he grabbed a pair of sweats from his drawer.

The look of confusion was evident on Cassie's face and he would have noticed it if he didn't have his back turned to her.

"What do you mean taking the heat off of you?" she wanted to know.

"If they hadn't arrested her then they would definitely be arresting me," he revealed nonchalantly.

"Why would they be arresting you?"

"Did we not just go to the hospital because my

wife and child are laid up there in a coma?"

"And?"

"And how do you think she ended up there?" he asked turning around to face her. It took her a minute for what he had said to register and when it did her mouth dropped open.

"No…you didn't…but why?" she asked confused. Nothing was making any sense to her. The man that she thought was this knight in shining armor was turning out to be something that she had never imagined. Was Trinity always getting abused or was this the first time and it just got out of hand? So many questions were forming in her brain but none of them could escape her mouth. She was frozen.

"Not that I owe you an explanation but I did it because she lied to me. All of these months I was thinking that I was going to have a son and come to find out that little bastard baby is a girl," he scoffed.

"Wait what? You beat her because the baby is a girl? It shouldn't matter what gender it is as long as it's healthy. You're her father for Christ's sake!" Cassie yelled getting up in his face.

Big mistake.

It was like in that second Dre changed into someone that she didn't know. Before she could make her feet listen to the command that her mind gave to run, he had his hand around her throat and had lifted her into the air. He slammed her body into the wall so hard that it shook. He continued to squeeze harder but not hard enough to cause her to pass out. At least not right away but if he didn't let go soon she might be passed out permanently.

Speaking through gritted teeth Dre made himself clear.

"If you ever raise your voice at me again I will rip your voice box out with my bare hands. And if I chose to beat my no good wife that's my business. She knows her place and you better know yours. What man wants to raise a little girl by a woman that has no morals? All she's gonna do is grow up to be a hoe like the woman that gave birth to her. Nah not me. So if she doesn't survive that's fine by me but if she does I won't be raising her. Now go clean yourself up and make me some breakfast then get out of my house," he spoke calmly before releasing her like she was a sack of potatoes.

Cassie felt like she was breathing in pure fire as she tried desperately to get the oxygen to her lungs that they craved. Her heart was beating so rapidly that she just knew at any moment it would explode in her chest. She watched Dre as he watched her before going into the bathroom and slamming the door. A few minutes passed by before she heard the shower turn on and that was her que to leave. If Dre wanted to eat he was going to have to fix it himself. She was leaving and never coming back she thought as she moved as quickly as she could to gather her things.

Just as she had opened the bedroom door the water turned off and she knew that she had to hurry before he caught her. His strength was that of twenty men and she wanted no parts of anymore of that.

"Cassie!" he shouted right as she made it to the front door. She could hear his heavy footsteps behind her as tears fell down her face.

Not bothering to look back she made it to her car right before he could catch her and immediately started it up. Her hands were shaking so bad but she managed to throw it into gear and high tail it out of the driveway as he stood watching her with a menacing smirk on his face. Something inside of her told her that this wouldn't be the last that he saw of her and that put the fear of God inside of her.

Looking over to the time on the dash she knew that Leron was probably at work or either church. She didn't know which one because she hadn't been home in almost three days. Her alibi would be Trinity and that she had been with her the entire time from the house to the hospital. It would be easy to make up a lie about what happened to her and have him believe her. But as she looked up into the mirror, she knew that it would be a daunting task of trying to explain the fingerprints that were now marking up her neck along with the passion marks from Dre.

-23-

Anya sat out on the balcony of her hotel room that overlooked the turquoise blue waters of the Dominican Republic. She was thinking about all that she had gone through over the years and where she was currently. The tests and trials that made her stronger, although some were harder than others, she was thankful for them now. Her relationship with God was stronger than ever, her career was thriving, and she finally had the man that was created specifically for her.

Bless was everything to Anya and it felt like they had been together for a lifetime already and she couldn't wait to spend many more with him. Not everyone was excited about them being together but Anya had learned a long time ago that she wasn't put on this earth to please people. Her heart was at peace knowing that she handled the situation the way that God needed her to and she was perfectly fine with that as long as Bless was. The last thing she wanted was for him to feel any regrets about being with her but since his eyes were open and he could see everything clearly now, he too was at peace.

"Hey best frannn," Ronda said startling her. She was so deep into her thoughts that she didn't even hear the door next to her balcony open.

"Hey sis and hey my punkin!" Anya exclaimed once she saw Ronda holding her daughter.

Reaching out for her Godmother, baby Anya smiled as wide as she could showing all three of her little teeth. Anya had only known Ronda and Terrell for such a short time before she went into labor and when she was asked to be one of their daughter's Godparents she was in shock but honored at the same time. Ronda was adamant that she knew God was telling her that Anya was the one she could trust for the position and Terrell agreed. The way baby Anya was trying her hardest to get over the rail to Anya let her know that she approved as well.

"Where y'all going all dressed up like it's Easter Sunday? I thought the afternoon service was kind of laid back as far as the dress code went" Anya asked.

Every year Bless' parents picked a different location for their annual church retreat and this year they decided to pick the Dominican Republic. Anya was so excited about going and couldn't wait to see what the beautiful country had to offer them. But first they had to attend their first service of the day. There had been so many things that she wanted to experience with Bless for the first time and she was thankful that this was one of them.

"You think this is too much?" Ronda asked looking down at what she was wearing.

She was dressed in a beautiful red strapless dress that stopped right below her knees and she had her daughter in a white dress that had flowers on the front. Her hair was pulled up into two long ponytails with white ribbons around them and Ronda's face had a natural beat to it. They looked gorgeous but a little too overdressed.

"Just a little. Mrs. Williams said to come comfortable and relaxed since the weather is nice and we will be outside. You don't want little mama getting fussy because she's too hot," Anya stated.

"You're right. Let me change her and then I will be over there in a few for you to help me pick something out."

"Ok the door is open."

Heading back inside to the room Ronda put an almost sleeping baby down on her bed as she grabbed the garment bag from the closet.

"You going to see Anya?" Terrell asked coming out of the bathroom.

"Yeah. It shouldn't take too long unless she takes forever," Ronda giggled.

"Well if she knows like I know she better hurry up before people start getting hungry. You know we can only go so long without eating before we catch an attitude and I'm almost there."

Laughing at her husband, she kissed him on the lips before promising to hurry up so that they could go. Her heart was beating so fast with excitement that she couldn't walk fast enough.

"What are you smiling so hard about over there?" Ronda inquired once she entered the room. Anya was still in the same spot outside that she was before with a faraway look in her eyes and a smile on her face.

"Sis I have never been this happy in my life. I finally feel like everything that God promised me I am receiving."

"Well boo that's what happens when you trust Him completely and hold on to what He told you. Too many times life can cause our faith to waver just when we need to hold on to it the most. We give up when we are the closest to our breakthrough because of what we see instead of holding on to what we have yet to see."

"That is so true but let's hurry up and get ready before we're late," Anya told her as she stood up. All she had to do was slip her own sundress on and she would be ready.

"Oh I'm already ready. It's you that needs to hurry up," Ronda said with a smirk causing Anya to have a look of confusion on her face.

"My dress is right here," Anya informed her. She

lifted the colorful floral print dress from the chair to show her.

"You're not wearing that," Ronda informed her.

"What's wrong with it?"

"Nothing is wrong with it. It just doesn't go with the occasion."

Ronda walked closer to Anya and when she was close Anya noticed the tears in her eyes. She didn't know what was going on but her mind was telling her that something was up.

"Here," was all that Ronda said before she handed over a single piece of paper.

Taking it from her hand Anya unfolded it and began to read.

Anya,

I'm never good at always expressing my feelings in words because I'm an action kind of man but today is different. Who knew that when you walked into the store for the first time a couple of years ago that we would end up here? You were my breath of fresh air when I felt like I was suffocating. You showed me what genuine love felt like when there was a time that I thought I knew what it was. I never want to lose the feeling that you give me and God has given me confirmation that I won't. I love you

Anya and if you would do me the honor of being my wife, today, I will spend the rest of my life making you the happiest woman on earth.

Bless

Anya looked up at Ronda to see tears falling down her pretty face that matched the ones that Anya shed. If someone asked her if she was shocked that would have been an understatement. She had so many emotions flooding her mind that she couldn't think straight.

"Is he serious?" was all that she could manage to get out.

Instead of responding to her, Ronda opened the garment bag that she was holding and unzipped it revealing one of the most beautiful dresses that she had ever seen. It was a form fitting white strapless dress that had beading all over it and flared out at the bottom. It was the same dress that Bless had caught her looking at once before and she couldn't believe that he had paid that much attention and gotten it for her.

"It's very real sis. You have twenty minutes to get dressed and meet your husband on the beach," Ronda informed her.

"Huh? Wait what? I thought we were having service," Anya asked confused. She moved quickly to take the dress out and begin to slip it on her body.

"We are having a service, your wedding," Ronda laughed at the look on her girl's face.

"I can't believe this."

"Well believe it. Bless planned everything, with my help of course, but this was all his idea. From the destination, to the dress, even the decorations. Your man did it all and he did it all for you. I don't mean to bring up Trinity but sis I knew he loved her but the way he loves you is so much deeper because the love is mutual. You love him just as much and that allows him to be able to give you his all because he knows that you love him for the man that he is and not for what he has."

"God knows I have loved that man since I was just a teenager and we had never even met face to face. I just knew."

Ronda reached out to hug her friend because she understood how she was feeling. The same way Anya felt about Bless was the same way that she felt about Terrell and that love had never died down. They may have had their spats here and there about little things but it was never anything that caused their love to change. As long as Anya and Bless continued to communicate there would be nothing that could tear their marriage apart. Or was it?

Knock. Knock.

"Come in," Ronda yelled out. She had just zipped up Anya's dress and was helping her place the flower in her thick curly hair.

"Oh my God you look gorgeous," they heard Kimmie say just above a whisper.

"Kimmie! What are you doing here?" Anya asked shocked. Over the past few months she, Ronda, and Kimmie had grown extremely close but she had no idea that she was in on the big secret too.

"You knew too?" Anya wanted to know.

"Of course and I wouldn't miss this for the world. Daddy is downstairs too," Kimmie revealed about Anya's boss. Her work family really was like her extended family and because she had no one else in her biological family there to support her they wanted to be there for her.

"Awww stop crying sis you're gonna mess up your makeup," Ronda laughed while she blotted the tears away and added just a little more bronzer where the tears had removed it.

"There we go. Just as flawless as usual."

Anya looked in the mirror and couldn't believe the woman that looked back at her. She had been through so many ups and downs in her life and God had finally placed her where she needed to be. She couldn't wait to become Mrs. Bless Williams and have him all to herself for the rest of her life.

As soon as they got into the lobby they saw Terrell standing there waiting on them.

"I'm going to let them know we're ready," Kimmie said before walking off towards the exit that led down to the beach.

"Dang sis you gonna have my brother skip this wedding and take you back upstairs looking like that," Terrell said causing Anya to blush.

"Oh she's definitely gonna be pregnant tonight," Ronda chimed in.

"Shut up!" Anya laughed at the two of them.

"Here," Terrell told her as he handed her a frame that was hidden behind his back. When Anya took it she almost broke down in tears.

The picture was of her adoptive father Reginald as he held her on the day that her adoption was finalized. As crazy as it may have sounded, she remembered that day like it was yesterday. The love and joy that they gave her was something that she had always wanted to give to her own children.

"We know he isn't here to give you away so Bless thought instead of you carrying flowers you could carry his picture as I give you away on your father's behalf. I would be honored if you would allow me to," Terrell spoke to her.

"Dang bae I just got her makeup together cause she was crying upstairs and here you go," Ronda fussed as she looked in her purse for some tissue.

"Y'all don't know how much this means to me."

"We do and that's why we want to make sure this day is one of the best days of your life."

Once they had gotten Anya ready a final time, Terrell linked his arm with hers and followed behind Ronda. They could hear the music begin to play when they got to the door and when she looked out Anya was speechless. Bless had decorated everything in red and white knowing that her favorite color was red and their backdrop was the beautiful ocean. There were red rose petals leading from the door where she stood all the way down to the altar.

Bless began singing an original song that he had written just for her that made her heart melt and the tears flow rapidly as she walked down to meet him. It was a song that expressed how he now knew of a genuine love and she was the one that showed it to him. By the time the ceremony was over there wasn't a dry eye surrounding them and speaking blessings over their marriage. His father had been the one to marry them unlike Bless' marriage to Trinity and that was something that he was grateful for.

-24-

Ernestine sat beside her daughter's bed praying that she would come out of her ordeal alive. She had always told her that her decisions could cost her her life if she wasn't careful but those warnings had fallen on deaf ears. They still didn't have much to go on about who had assaulted Trinity and the police were in desperate need of information. Ernestine on the other hand had a feeling who was behind it though, she just couldn't prove it. But one thing she did know was that everything done in the dark God would surely bring it to the light and her so called husband was going to have some explaining to do.

Dre may have had Trinity fooled but Ernestine and Jessie were smarter than that. He had all of the material things that their daughter craved and that was a dangerous thing. He had blinded her from the truth but she would bet everything she had that he was behind Trinity laying in that bed fighting to survive.

"You still here?"

Ernestine looked up to see Dre standing there with a smug look on his face. If she had to picture what Satan looked like the man before her would be it. He was handsome and built but his attitude made him so ugly to her. She could understand why her child had fallen for him because they were definitely one in the same. As beautiful as Trinity was on the outside her attitude and character made her so ugly.

"Why wouldn't I be?" Ernestine inquired.

"I just figured that you would rather be down at that church that you love so much saving souls and caring about others more than your own child. I mean isn't that what you have been doing her whole life?"

"Baby don't come up in here thinking you know me when you don't. If anything her father and I have sacrificed so much for her little ungrateful behind and never once did we put anyone before her. She was the one who decided to go against the grain and look where that has gotten her," Ernestine gritted as she pointed to the bed.

"Sounds like the typical holy roller reply. Always pretending someone else is to blame."

Dre had only met Trinity's parents once since they had been together and that was after they got married. He knew that if she was his wife then there wasn't much that they could say to make her leave him. Trinity was too down for him to but he still wasn't taking any chances. The second her parents laid eyes on him he could already tell they disapproved and he knew how. He may not have gone to church or even believed in half of what they taught but he did know that people could pick up on another person. Just like he had read Trinity on the flight that he met her on and knew that she was easy, her parents saw right past his clean cut exterior and saw him for the callous individual that he really was.

"You can call it what you want to but we both know the truth. Too bad my daughter may not make it out of this before it's revealed to her. But make no mistake about it, your days are numbered too baby," she warned him before grabbing her purse and heading towards the door. Just as she was about to open it Cassie came through in a hurry.

"Baby there are-," she began before stopping dead in her tracks at the sight of her aunt.

"Baby?" Ernestine asked with her brows raised. There was no way that her niece was calling her son-in-law baby. She may have known the type of woman that Cassie was because she was her niece, but never in her life would she have thought Cassie would stoop that low.

"Oh hey auntie…what are you doing here? Um I was talking to Leron," Cassie lied.

"Really? Where is he then?" Ernestine asked as she stuck her head out into the hallway. Just like she thought Leron wasn't behind her.

"Auntie I need you to get with the times. I was

talking to him on my blue tooth."

Cassie quickly pointed to the device that was hanging around her neck to further prove her lie. From the way that her aunt was looking at her she didn't know if it was believable or not but she was hoping that it was. There was no way that she wanted anyone to find out about her messing around with her cousin's husband.

Instead of responding, Ernestine gave them both a knowing look before walking out of the room to go and check on her granddaughter in the NICU. She prayed that somehow Trinity had gotten pregnant by Bless and that was his child but the moment she saw that little yellow bald headed baby she knew that Dre was her father. Any hope of her having a normal parent was down the drain because they were both unfit in her opinion.

"You know that was close right?" Dre asked invading Cassie's space.

"Too close. But there's a cop outside talking to one of the nurses. I couldn't make out what he was saying though."

"Don't stress that. They have nothing on me that connects me to this," he told her confidently while licking his lips.

Cassie knew that this shouldn't be happening especially with her cousin in the bed beside them but there was just something about Dre that she couldn't resist. Even if he did choke her the other day. When he called her later on that same night, after her husband had gone to sleep, he apologized to her and explained that he was just under a lot of pressure. But she wasn't back with him just because he had apologized to her, she had something that she needed to tell him.

"Dre baby we need to talk right quick," she did her best to tell him. The way his kisses felt on her neck and his hand was sliding up her shirt was sending her body into a frenzy.

"Shhh," he whispered while guiding her towards the bathroom.

"She's in there?" Cassie almost shrieked.

"So what? She can't hear us and if she could what would she do?" he stated with not a care in the world.

"Mmmm," Cassie moaned out in ecstasy as a single tear leaked from Trinity's eye.

***

It was a little after three in the afternoon when Cassie pulled into her driveway. She knew that Leron wasn't supposed to be home until around 8pm due to him going on a day trip with a few of the other brothers at their church. That gave her time to shower and get the remnants of her escapade off of her body and start dinner. The last thing she wanted to do was raise any red flags with him. Lately she felt like she had been slipping and although he never said anything to her. Still she wanted to make sure she was extra careful. She had a feeling that the day she came home with the hickeys and fingermarks around her neck that he suspected something was up, but the concealer that she had managed to cake on saved her from having to lie any more than she already had. It was odd that Leron believed her lie a little too fast about being at the hospital for three days but she just figured that he trusted her. Besides she had never given him reason not to.

Looking around her car she made sure that there

was nothing out of place or any reminders of what she had done in sight. There had been a few times when they couldn't wait to get to his house or a hotel room and her car had to accommodate them. Leron rarely drove her car but she wasn't taking any chances. After making sure that everything was in place she got out and headed inside.

Cassie unlocked the door and quickly shut it behind her before going into the kitchen. She was moving so fast to get things in order for dinner that she didn't feel the presence behind her.

"In a hurry?" Leron asked startling her and causing Cassie to drop the package of ground beef on the floor.

"Hey baby! Goodness you scared me." The shaking was evident in her voice but she tried her best to hide it with a smile on her face.

"Where have you been?" he asked. The tone in his voice wasn't the usual chipper one that she had grown used to. It was calmer than usual with an undertone of anger that made her sick to her stomach. Did he know something about what she had been doing? There was no way that he could know because she had been so careful.

"I was at the hospital with Trin and the baby. She's so cute and tiny Ron. You have got to go see her," Cassie tried easing the tension in the kitchen.

"I already have," he said shocking her.

"Really? When?"

"Earlier today before the fellowship with the brothers. My spirit led me to go and pray for them."

"Well that was nice baby but why didn't you tell me and I could have met you up there?"

"It was last minute and I had a few errands to run. So is there anything you want to tell me?" Leron asked.

"Not that I can think of." Cassie didn't know what he was getting at but she was starting to feel uneasy. Out of all the years that she had been with her husband he had never made her feel the fear that was taking over her body. Something wasn't right but she was too scared to ask.

"So you weren't going to tell me about these?" he asked as he pulled a bottle of pills from his pocket. Cassie's stomach dropped to her knees and it probably would have hit her feet if her knees weren't already knocking together in fear.

"What are those?" she asked knowing full well what they were. He was holding her prenatal vitamins that she had recently picked up.

"When were you going to tell me that we were having a baby?" Leron exclaimed with a smile as wide as a mile long. Before she could register what was taking place he had crossed the room and lifted her up into his arms as he held her close.

The motion from him swinging her and the nervousness that she was feeling a few seconds before was enough to make her puke all over the floor but she held it together. She had found out that she was pregnant only two weeks before and she hadn't quite thought of a way to tell him about the baby. Cassie knew how much he missed his children with his ex-wife because Heather wouldn't allow him to see them. She was still hurt and bitter and used his children against him. Cassie had been trying to get pregnant for the longest and when it finally happened she was ecstatic. She felt like the baby would be the one who could get her back in Leron's pockets and she could leave her man on the side alone for good. She was a First Lady for Christ's sake and had an image to uphold. With their anniversary coming up that would be the perfect time to tell him but the cat was now out of the bag.

"I was waiting to surprise you for our anniversary but since you had to go snooping, you're going to be a daddy!"

Leron continued to hold her but the longer he did the harder he began to squeeze. In comparison to her small frame Leron was almost a foot taller than she was and had her by a good hundred and fifty pounds. He may have been caught up in being happy about the news but she was miserable in that moment and felt like she couldn't breathe.

"You know Cass, I wish I could believe that but since I had a vasectomy almost ten years ago I find it hard to believe that child you are carrying is mine," he revealed.

If God had never heard any of her prayers before, Cassie prayed that he would hear her now and take her on to glory. Shoot after all she had done in life He probably wouldn't let her in but she asked anyway. Nothing after what Leron said could salvage her marriage and she knew that it was over. Her conniving and scheming ways had finally caught up to her. Everything that her family had told both her and Trinity were coming true and she was going to have to live with that.

"I'm pretty sure that Trinity would be upset knowing that you were pregnant by her husband. But since she has made her own bed and is literally lying in it, that may be punishment enough. Too bad you won't be here to find out," he said sending a cold chill down her spine.

What did he mean she wouldn't be there to find out? Where was she going and how in the world did he know about Dre? Before she could ask either of those questions he gave her those answers and more.

"You know what, you cost me everything. My wife, my children, my church. I knew the minute you walked in there I should have done an exorcism to get those demons out of you. I saw those spirits just as clear as day and so did Heather but I was weak. I thought about the one thing that my wife wasn't doing instead of all of the things that she was and I let that cloud my judgement. By then it was too late. I let my sexual frustrations take over and thought that what we had was love but I was wrong. So, so wrong. All you wanted was my money but baby girl you seem to have underestimated me.

See, I knew that if the money would stop then the way you were treating me would stop so I paid attention. The late nights, days away from home, oh and let's not forget about the hickeys that were on your neck a while back," he said catching her totally off guard.

Cassie's body immediately stiffened up at the mention of those marks. How could she have been so stupid to even come home right after that but she had no other options at that moment. It was either go home or stay and deal with Dre and his temper.

"Baby I'm sorry."

"Shut up! You're sorry alright. A sorry excuse for a wife and a woman but that's ok. I won't dare let a child be born into this world with you as a mother," he continued.

Leron loosened his grip just a little so that he could turn around and walk towards the basement steps and that one slip up allowed Cassie to break free. She hadn't gotten two steps away from him before she felt like her head was set on fire from the ripping of her hair from her scalp.

"Ahhhhh!" she screamed hoping that one of her neighbors could hear her.

Finally getting her under control somewhat, Leron dragged her down the steps by her hair making sure that her body hit every one of the concrete steps.

"I realize now how selfish I was and it cost me the love of my life and our children. I left a good woman for one that wasn't bout nothing all because I couldn't control my flesh. My kids hate me because of you!" he yelled throwing her down the rest of the way.

Cassie hit the floor with a thud causing her to temporarily become dazed. She could hear him moving around but her vision was too blurry to make out exactly what he was doing until she heard the familiar click of a gun whose safety had just been released.

"No please Ron baby. I'm so sorry. Please just let me go and I will stay far away from you. You don't have to worry about me anymore," Cassie cried.

"I can't do that love. See I may not have honored my vows the first time but I will this go round. We vowed to be together 'til death do us part and we will. I have nothing else to live for anyway."

Pow! Pow!

Cassie felt the impact of the two bullets as they entered her chest. She prayed that God would forgive her for all of the many sins that she had committed and asked to be received by Him before hearing another shot ring out. The sickening sound of Leron's dead body hitting the ground beside her let her know that he had indeed honored his vows of 'til death do them part. As she closed her eyes and welcomed her fate she remembered one scripture.

Leviticus 20:10, If a man commits adultery with the wife of his neighbor, both the adulterer and the adulteress shall surely be put to death.

-25-

Trinity sat on her sofa looking down into the face of her daughter with so much on her mind. She was finally understanding what it meant that you reap what you sow. For as long as she could remember she never worried about her actions coming back on her but now her luck had run out. If she could go back and do things over she would. It was crazy how one decision a person made could hurt so many others in life. Looking down into her gorgeous daughter's face it hit her that what she had done back in high school was now going to affect her child and that was an eye opener.

Giselle Renee spent the first twelve days of her life without her mother because Trinity was selfish. She cared more about herself than anyone else even her own child. Had she taken the time to think about her first born Trinity would have realized that she needed to make things right and get far away from Dre. It was because of her selfishness that they both almost lost their lives yet God spared them both.

Placing Giselle in her bassinet she pushed her towards the kitchen so that she could prepare what she planned to be Dre's last home cooked meal. After what she had heard going on in the hospital bathroom between he and Cassie she was ready to send him on his way. Never again would she put a man or material things before what was really important. She and Cassie may have been low down when it came to decisions in their lives but never would she have expected her own flesh and blood to do her so dirty. Trinity figured that either Cassie knew something was up or she had a guilty conscious and that was why she had been ignoring Trinity's calls. She had been blowing up her phone so much and leaving messages for her to call back that her mailbox was now full. Trinity didn't sweat it though because after she dealt with Dre, Cassie was next on her list.

The beeping from the garage door signaled Dre's arrival. Ever since she had gotten home the only time he would be there was to shower and change and head back out. She couldn't stop herself from wondering if he was going to spend time with her cousin instead of being there with her and their new baby. It was funny how she was now feeling the same way that Bless had felt when she was doing the exact same thing to him.

Bless. God knows that man had loved her unconditionally and Trinity felt bad for the things that she had done to him. She may have never loved him the way that he loved her but she did indeed care for him. He didn't deserve to be treated the way that she had treated him and she hoped that one day he could forgive her.

Hearing the interior door that led from the garage snapped Trinity out of her thoughts and focused on her husband. Dre was still one of the most handsome men that she had ever been with but now that she knew the real him none of that mattered. As soon as Dre stepped inside he halted his stride smelling something that was unfamiliar to him. Following the aroma he walked in on Trinity standing over a pot of fresh collard greens which were his favorite. Out of all the time that he had known her she had never lifted a finger to cook so this was something new. Maybe the beating he gave her knocked some sense into her after all and she was finally being whipped into shape just the way he liked.

"What's all of this?" he asked.

"Well I figured with everything going on recently you would just want a night to relax and enjoy a home cooked meal," she smiled.

Instead of responding he walked over to the fridge in search for an ice-cold beer. After the day that he had trying to reach Cassie and her not answering he couldn't think straight. During all of his meetings that he was holding with potential clients he couldn't focus because he was wondering where she was. It didn't matter though because as soon as he saw her he was going to make her regret not answering his calls. If she kept it up he would just have to make an appearance down to her little church to make himself known.

"Where is my beer?" Dre asked moving items around like that would somehow make one appear.

Trinity had forgotten to pick him up some more because Giselle had been fussy all morning. When he had sent her the text with his request of two cases of Heineken, it had totally slipped her mind. She didn't understand why he couldn't go get it himself considering she had a brand-new baby at home that she had to take care of but she would never say that to him. Trinity already knew that this slip up could cost her another beating and her body couldn't take anymore.

"I'm sorry baby but Giselle has been fussy all night and this morning so it slipped my mind. Besides I didn't want to take her out in that cool air," she tried explaining.

Looking over towards where Giselle slept peacefully, Dre looked at his daughter with a scowl on his face. He didn't think that it was possible for a person to hate someone more than he hated the daughter that he created. Just knowing that she would grow up to be just like both his and her trifling mothers sent him into a frenzy knocking the beautiful pink and white bassinet over onto the floor. It was in that moment that her loud piercing screams ignited something inside of Trinity and she rushed to get her baby off the floor.

She checked all over Giselle's little body and thankfully when the bassinet was knocked over she remained inside somehow. She was crying more from being startled than being hurt but Trinity didn't care. As soon as she was quiet again and she had placed her baby back inside of her bed she turned to Dre.

"Why did you do that? You could have killed our daughter."

"If she had died the first time then we wouldn't even be having this conversation. I don't care about that little bit-," Dre began to rant only to be cut off by the scalding sensation that he was feeling on his face and upper body.

"I hate you!" Trinity screamed as she continued using the now empty pot that contained the greens as a weapon. She didn't know where she had finally gotten the strength to fight back but now that she had there was nothing that was going to stop her. She was going to release all of the hurt, fear, and anger that she had felt right on him. Trinity may have made many mistakes in her life but now that she was a mother herself she finally understood how her mother tried to protect her. Giselle would never have to worry about anyone hurting her if Trinity had anything to do with it.

Dre tried his best to fight back but the way the pain

was taking over his body he was definitely on the losing end. He imagined that what he was feeling was how all of the women he had ever laid hands on felt but most of all he thought about how his mother felt when his father beat her. The agony he felt at the memories of his father telling him that was how all women should be treated and if they bucked the system, beat them harder. That's why he wanted to have a son. There was no way that he could live knowing that one day his daughter could possibly be on the receiving end of a man's fist.

The way Trinity was going in on him he wished that his mother would have been that strong to fight his father. Instead she ran away and left him as a young child instead of taking him with her. True enough his father never laid a hand on him and he made sure that he had gotten everything that he wanted but he missed his mother. She may not have been able to teach him how to be a man but neither had his father. All he learned was how to be was an abuser.

"You tried killing me and our baby you bastard! I hate the day that I met you and as God as my witness if I ever see you again I will kill you," Trinity continued to yell with each blow before she was lifted from behind.

"It's ok baby girl Daddy's here," she heard her father Jessie say from behind her as she snapped out of the rage that she was in and broke down crying.

"Oh my God my babies!" Ernestine cried checking on Trinity and then reaching for Giselle who had been crying the entire time.

"Whoa!" the officer from the hospital said entering the house. He immediately ran over to where Dre was lying barely conscious and hurriedly read him his rights before he blacked out. He placed a call for an ambulance before standing up and checking on Trinity.

"Are you taking me to jail too?" she asked before he could speak. She had finally calmed down knowing that her parents were there and she and her baby were now safe.

"It was self-defense, right?"

Looking at the name on his badge she saw that his last name was Harper before speaking. She didn't know if she had to be careful about what she said because she watched too many crime shows and knew that anything she said could possibly be twisted and used against her. But the way that he was looking at her made her feel like she could be honest.

"Officer Harper he knocked my baby on the floor and I lost it. I thought about all the times that he beat me, especially when we almost died, and I blacked out. Whatever charges I will have to face I'm fine with as long as I can make sure that Giselle is alright," she let him know.

"No need for that," he said while shaking his head. "We have all of the evidence we need against him in order to justify this. No charges will be filed against you I can promise."

"How can you be so sure? I burned him with a pot of greens and he will be scarred for life."

"Look at it as that's his punishment for the scars that you and so many other women have to live with for the rest of your lives. That will be his daily reminder. You and that beautiful baby girl could have died at the hands of him and no judge is going to take that lightly. Besides we have his confession on tape."

Shocked Trinity looked over at her mother and back at her father who was still holding her with confusion in her eyes.

"When you were brought in to the hospital and he finally decided to arrive he wasn't alone. He was with your cousin. I watched the way he interacted with the doctor after finding out your condition and how the two of them looked closer than they should have been. I felt like something was up so I waited around until your parents arrived. I let them know my concerns and asked if they would mind helping me. When they agreed, I placed a hidden camera in you and your daughter's rooms and waited. We finally heard something that we could use," Officer Harper explained stopping just short of telling Trinity everything. He didn't know what headspace she was in and he didn't want to upset her any more than she already was.

"You heard him admit to beating me, Cassie saying she falsely accused Anya, and then them having sex in the bathroom because they thought I was unconscious."

With a sigh, Officer Harper nodded his head as he looked at her in her eyes with sympathy. For her to have heard everything made him feel even sorrier than before. No one should have to ever endure such things at the hands of the people who claim to love you. That was one reason why he had yet to marry. When he did he wanted it to be his first and his last.

"Possible murder suicide at 326 Dalton Ct," they heard coming through Harper's radio just as the medics arrived.

He turned around to cuff Dre to the stretcher before allowing the EMTs to head out the door as Trinity stood frozen in place. The address that was called out was one that she knew all too well.

"Oh God," was all that she could get out.

"What's wrong?" Ernestine and Jessie asked her at the same time. The fear and sorrow that was etched across her face alarmed not only them but Harper as well.

"Trinity are you alright?" he inquired.

"That's Cassie's address!"

-26-

It was the last night of Anya and Bless' honeymoon and neither of them were ready to return home. The peace that they had felt the whole time they had been together was nothing like either of them had ever experienced. Making Anya his life was one of the best decisions that Bless had ever made and unlike when he first married Trinity, there were no second thoughts.

The two of them had just made their way back to their room when Bless' phone began to ring. No one had bothered them the whole time they were gone so he knew that something had to be wrong if his mother was calling.

"Hey pretty lady," he greeted her.

"Hey baby," she replied sounding sad.

"Mama what's wrong?" Bless asked.

Anya stopped getting her things ready for their shower and looked towards him. She wasn't sure what was going on but the look on his face told her that it was deep. Bless listened intently as Anya waited to hear what was going on. After about ten minutes of just listening, he blew out a deep breath and finally sat on the edge of the bed with a solemn look on his face before speaking.

"Wow I don't know what to say. That's heavy

ma," he told her while gesturing for Anya to come to him. Once she got close he pulled her down on to his lap and caressed her side softly.

Just like that Anya temporarily forgot that something major was going on back home and she got caught up in his touch. For the first few days after they were married they found themselves holed up in their room. When God said that the marriage bed was undefiled they went all out. The connection that they had was incredible and nothing like either had ever had the pleasure of experiencing. It was like Bless knew her body and she knew his and because of that Anya knew that it wouldn't take long for her to get pregnant if they kept that up.

"Um Cassie is dead," she heard Bless say.

"Wait…what?"

"Apparently, she was sleeping with Dre behind both her husband and Trinity's backs and Leron may have found out. They found the two of them shot in their basement with a gun still in his hand."

"Are you serious?"

"Yeah. Somehow her parents found out that Dre was the one who had beat Trinity so bad and when they went to the house with the officer she was in there beating him with a hot pot of greens. Burned him up real bad."

As horrible as it sounded, part of Anya wanted to giggle because all she could picture was when Madea taught her niece how to play grit ball in one of Tyler Perry's movies.

"Did she get arrested?"

"Nah. It was justified especially after she told them that he had knocked their baby on to the floor."

"Oh God no! Is the baby alright?"

"She was just a little shaken up but nothing more. Anyway while they were there a call came through about a possible murder suicide and Trinity immediately recognized the address as Cassie's. So, they went to her house just to make sure and that's where they found them. A UPS worker had gone to the house to deliver a package and noticed the door open and a strong stench coming from the inside. He called the police and they ended up determining they had been in the basement for at least a week."

"Dang that long? Lord that's so sad."

"I agree. I mean I never really cared for her but I wouldn't wish anything like that on anyone. But I mean you cannot escape the consequences of one's actions. No matter how long after that seed has been sown, good or bad, you can believe that you will reap a harvest. That's why we should stop living in the moment and not thinking about the consequences and be careful of the choices we make. Cassie and Trinity made some bad decisions that unfortunately caused one to be near death and the other to experience death. I just pray that they both have repented of their sins and asked for true forgiveness," Bless said pulling her close and kissing her exposed arm.

Anya knew exactly what he was saying was true and she prayed that the decisions that she made in her past wouldn't come back to haunt her in the same way that Cassie had to deal with.

"You ok baby?" Bless asked noticing that she had gotten unusually quiet.

"Hmm? Oh yeah. Let's get showered and relaxed so we don't miss our flight in the morning."

"If you bless me tonight like you have been for the last two weeks then we might need to change our flight," Bless told her as he reached out to grab her around her waist. Giggling she broke free before running into the bathroom with her husband hot on her heels.

Epilogue

Anya looked out into the backyard and watched her husband running around with their son Malcolm. The joy that was evident on his face and that filled her heart with so much joy. Never in a million years did she think that this would be her life. Here she was married to her first love, they both owned their own business that provided well for their family, and they shared a beautiful son with another on the way. Life for them was indeed blessed and she couldn't have been happier.

She tore her eyes from the backyard when she heard the front door open followed by the laughter of her three-year-old God daughter who was also her namesake.

"Little girl slow down before you fall," Ronda called out behind her.

"Tee Tee!" Anya screamed ignoring her mother and running into the arms of the woman who was like her second mother.

"Hey my baby girl!"

"Yook."

Anya looked down at the shirt that she was wearing and noticed that it had a #1 on the front with

Malcom's name and a dump truck on the front. It was her son's first birthday and she thought that it was so cute that everyone made it their business to make it all about him. She couldn't do too much because she had been sick lately but between Bless, Ronda and Terrell, and her parents everything she needed and wanted for her little man had gotten done.

"I love your shirt An. How about you go and show it to your God brother and daddy," Anya said putting her down so that she could run off.

"Here is your shirt and one for Bless," Terrell said passing one off to her and quickly going behind his daughter before she jumped off the back porch. That little girl was a daredevil and kept them on their toes but he loved it.

"So you invite everybody?" Ronda asked. She began washing her hands so that she could help prep the food for the grill before the guests began to arrive.

"Yeah I did," Anya replied. She already knew what Ronda was asking and that was if she had invited Trinity.

As crazy as it may have sounded, Anya had no hate towards Trinity. All of the hurt that she caused everyone had finally come back to her and it made her really open her eyes. With her near death experience and the death of her cousin she looked at life totally different.

Because of that Anya was able to accept her apology when she showed up to their house months after she and Bless had married. They weren't the best of friends but they were cordial. Besides Anya had no worries about Trinity wanting Bless anymore now that she had finally found the man that God had intended for her. Officer Harper had come along during the most trying time of her life and she welcomed him into her life. They were now engaged and he treated her daughter Giselle like his own.

"Sis I have to give it to you. You are much better at forgiveness than I am cause babyyyy if it was me, you already know that every time I saw her she would catch these hands!"

"Lord you so dramatic," Anya laughed before yawning.

"You haven't taken a nap have you?" Ronda asked.

"No I've been ripping and running all day making sure I had everything together."

"Well go take a quick nap and we will make sure that everything is done. You have about another two hours before everyone gets here so you have time."

"You sure sis?"

The look that Ronda gave her let her know that she

was not about to play with her and that she had better go do as she was told. Kissing her best friend on the cheek she made her way to the master bedroom. Kicking off her flats, Anya stepped up on the stool and laid across her bed. Her life was far from perfect but it was also far from where it used to be. Because of that she was thankful and couldn't wait to see what the future held for her and her family.

Bless laughed as he chased his son around the yard. It was Malcom's first birthday and they had gone all out for his party. He had been wanting a child for so long and when they found out Anya had gotten pregnant on their honeymoon they were both elated. Now here they were about to have another child, a daughter, and he was on top of the world.

"Gotcha!" Bless called out as he grabbed his giggling child up into his arms.

"Unkyyyy!" Malcolm called out once he caught his breath and saw Terrell coming through the back door.

"Nephewwww!" Terrell called back in the same playful manner. It warmed his heart every time he saw his best friend with his son. To know all of the things that Bless had gone through to get to this moment, made him praise the God he served even more.

"What's going on bro? Hey my princess," Bless reached out for little Anya as she grabbed his legs.

"Hi Uncle Bless," Anya said squeezing him as tight as her little arms could before she and Malcolm ran off to play on the bounce house that was set up.

"Ronda just made sis go lay down cause she looked like she was about to fall over any minute."

"It's about time. That woman has been in overdrive all morning with her beautiful self," Bless smiled as he thought about his queen.

"I can tell. Well tell me what you need help with so that we can get my lil' man's day going before his aunt comes out here to inspect," Terrell laughed as the two of them got ready to spend another of many birthdays together.

The End… or is it?

***

Looking around the church made Anya sick. All of those people in there with their heads thrown back and hands held high screaming out the highest praise.

"Hallelujah!"

"Thank ya Jesus!"

They were a mess and she wasn't here for it. Anya loved the Lord and didn't mind coming to give Him praise but knowing the things that she knew caused her to want to be far away. There was too much on her mind and she had no idea how she was going to make it out.

"Babe you alright?" her boyfriend Rico asked coming up behind her right before it was time to take up the last offering.

"Just a slight headache coming on," she told him. God was going to have to forgive her for that lie later.

"Well you should go on home then and lay down. We should be done in a few and I can stop and pick you something up to eat on the way. I know my little one is being difficult tonight," he smiled as he ran his hand across her slightly pudgy stomach.

"I think that's what I'll do. Don't be long ok?" she said to him as she gently kissed his cheek.

The kiss of death.

"You leaving already?" First Lady Brenda asked walking up behind them. It never failed that whenever

they were together she was always somewhere lurking.

"Yea my little man is giving Anya a hard time tonight," Rico smiled hard.

The look that flashed across her face may have gone unnoticed by her boyfriend but not Anya. Some would think that after almost three years in a relationship her man would have that all figured out but she guessed he was still thinking with his little head instead of the one on his shoulders.

"Well you better get some rest. We won't be too much longer," she said before walking off.

First Lady Brenda Mason was a bad woman. Her long brown hair that was never out of place framed her pretty almond colored face and she had one of the sickest bodies ever. All of the men in the church had a hard time keeping their eyes off of her but their wives would kindly assist them when needed. Anya's boyfriend on the other hand, knew how to keep his eyes in check. Well at least to the unknowing people he did. Every moved that Rico made was calculated but unfortunately so were hers.

Being that he was a deacon he had to be one of the last ones to leave the church so that gave Anya just enough time to do what she was told to do. Speaking to a few of the members on the way out of the church she headed to Rico's car.

Jumping on the expressway it took me only a few minutes for her to get to her destination. She was shaking like a leaf and tried to think of everything that could get her out of the bind she was in unscathed.

Parking a few streets over and since it had already gotten dark outside she hoped that she could go undetected. She changed from the all-white suit that she had been wearing and put on her skinny jeans and tank top. Anya unpinned her hair and let it fall around her shoulders before grabbing her "peace be still" that she had been given and hopped out.

Backtracking towards the house she entered the back and waited to make sure the alarm had already been disabled. After listening for the beep to come Anya walked over to the kitchen counter and popped the bottle of Barefoot Moscato that was available. She was indeed pregnant but since the doctor told her that she could have a glass of wine a day she took it to the head. Her OB/GYN just didn't say how big the glass should to be.

The sound of a car door shutting brought her back to her task. Running up the stairs she headed straight for the closet in the master bedroom. The blinds on the door were already open just right to where she could see out but no one could see in.

"Come on baby hurry up!" she heard Rico say.

The only response to his request was a moan and she was well aware of who that belonged to. For the last year, the two of them had been having an affair. They thought that since no one had called them out on it that they were safe. It started with a little flirting, then came the requests to help around the church more, then going on trips that the Pastor couldn't attend because he was booked for other events. But it was now time for their sins to be revealed.

She waited a few minutes until she heard that faithful grunt and knew that Rico was near his happy place.

"Should I wait until you're done or can we get this show on the road?" Anya asked coming out of the closet. She may have sounded calm but on the inside she was shaking like a leaf. She was about to do something that she knew was wrong but her hands were tied. It was either them or her.

"Baby? W-w-what are you doing here?" Rico stuttered as Brenda tried to cover herself up.

"Girl ain't no need for all of that hollering," Anya told her rolling her eyes.

"It's not what you think."

"Oh I know that. See what I thought was that the man I had fallen in love with wouldn't turn out like my no good daddy and treat me like my mama was treated," Anya lied keeping her eyes on Trinity.

"Come on baby we can work this out. Let me get dressed and we can go home and talk this out. God will get us through this," he tried convincing her. The sound that came from behind Anya was unfamiliar even to her. The laugh was sinister and from the looks on the both of their faces she knew that it had chilled them to the bone.

No other words needed to be said between anyone

because she was sure that they both knew their end was near. Whatever conversation Rico wanted to have with God he could have it face to face before he received his judgement.

POW! POW!

Both bodies lay side by side as an arm pulled me close.

"Come on baby our plane is ready."

***

Inmate 63-8912005

"Crawford!" the burly guard called out.

This was the day that Nardo Crawford had been waiting for. Seven years, ten months, and three weeks he had been waiting on his release and it was finally there. He dapped up his boys that he had been locked up with and grabbed the few items that he had. Because everyone left him out to dry when he got knocked there was no money that was put on his books regularly to get the things he needed. Once in a blue moon one of his old flames would drop a couple of dollars his way. All of the other times he had to get it how he lived but that was all coming to an end.

It took him a little over an hour to process out and his anxiety was beginning to get the best of him. Nardo kept looking at the clock and watching the guards as he bounced his leg impatiently. After a few more minutes he was finally called to the window to sign his papers and receive the few dollars that the jail gave out and a bus ticket. Walking out of those gates and waiting for the bus to transport him away from that hell hole and to the bus station, all Nardo could think about was what was to come.

Everyone abandoned him when he needed them the most especially the woman that he thought was down to ride for him until the very end. She may have been living it up and thought she was free and clear but just as soon as he was on his feet again he would be right back to reign terror in her life. Anya better enjoy it while she could because all of her hidden secrets were about to be exposed.

Stay tuned for the spinoff "Beautiful Sins: Anya's Deception!

CPSIA information can be obtained
at www.ICGtesting.com
Printed in the USA
LVOW13s2344250518
578521LV00010B/413/P